WE COULD'VE BEEN Happy HERE

STORIES

KEITH LESMEISTER

D0063530

MG
PRESS

In memory of JPL.

ADVANCE PRAISE

A gritty, emotionally sensitive clutch of stories."
—Kirkus Reviews

The Middlewesterners in Keith Lesmeister's charming collection We Could've Been Happy Here share more in common with Ethan and Joel Coen's Fargo than any of Willa Cather's stalwart pioneers. But these characters and their stories are perfectly authentic, hilarious, and offbeat. This collection is the genuine article.
—Nickolas Butler, author of *Shotgun Lovesongs* and *The Hearts of Men*

"There's a tricky playfulness to Keith Lesmeister's fiction. His characters are painfully flawed—but their goodness always shines through. And his humor lights up the page—but it's so often a trapdoor to the sadness that unifies these stories. *We Could've Been Happy Here* is a lovely heartache of a collection."
—Benjamin Percy, author of *The Dead Lands, Red Moon, Thrill Me, The Wilding* and *Refresh, Refresh*

"Once in a great while, you pick something up, and its great, subtle beauty hits you slowly and hard like the wave of an ocean. That's the case for *We Could've Been Happy Here*, except the ocean is in Iowa. I've lived in the world that Lesmeister is showing us for over a decade, and the people who inhabit this collection are strange and sad and unique, and deeply familiar; I hurt for them. Collections like this only come around once in a while."
—Erika T. Wurth, author of *Crazy Horse's Girlfriend*

"The deceptively quiet stories in Keith Lesmeister's *We Could've Been Happy Here* lay bare the inner lives of deceptively ordinary people in the deceptively normative state of Iowa. Like a heartland Chekhov, Lesmeister artfully refuses to tell us how things turned out—did that slacker stay sober? did that nice middle-aged couple who robbed a bank on a lark ever get caught? Instead, he reveals how things are in his characters' souls: often strange and dark, yet not without hope and love."
—**David Gates**, author of *Preston Falls* and *A Hand Reached Down to Guide Me*

"These are brutal stories—brutally good, brutally urgent, brutally hopeful. In this extraordinary collection, Keith Lesmeister has granted his lucky readers a rare and stirring look into the soul of the middle west. His prose is as clean as the prairie wind, his characters as dangerous and refreshing as summer storms. *We Could've Been Happy Here* is a real achievement, a book that won't let you go and you're all the better for it."
—**Bret Anthony Johnson**, author of *Remember Me Like This* and *Corpus Christi: Stories*

WE COULD'VE BEEN

Happy

HERE

STORIES

To Rosanna —
Thanks for
your support!
Enjoy
Keith

MG Press
http://midwestgothic.com/mgpress

Some stories originally appeared in the following publications: "Nothing Prettier Than This" (*Gettysburg Review*, Fall 2015), "Today You're Calling Me Lou" (*Meridian*, Winter 2014), "Lie Here Next to Me" (*Tishman Review*, Winter 2017), "Imaginary Enemies" (*American Short Fiction*, Spring 2014), "Burrowing Animals" (*Redivider*, Winter 2014), "Company & Companionship" (*Columbia Review*, Spring 2015), "Blood Trail" (*Harpur Palate,* Fall 2014), "East of Ely" (*Flyway*, Summer 2015), "We Could've Been Happy Here" (*Slice Magazine*, Fall 2015).

ISBN: 978-1-944850-05-0

Cover design © 2017 Lauren Crawford

Author photo © Celia Lesmeister

NOTHING
PRETTIER
THAN
THIS

I'd been farm-sitting out at Lyle's for less than a day. This was late October, an Indian summer worth remembering. I'd brought along knitting supplies and a girl I used to know named Katharine. She was married to this guy, Ted, who had no clue she was there. She leaned against a fence post with the sun on her face, lighting her up like some ancient piece of liturgical artwork.

"Those bitches are never coming back," Katharine said. She was referring to the cows. She was younger than me, maybe twenty-nine.

"Have hope," I said. I put the emphasis on hope in a knowing way, and I got the response I was looking for. She smirked, shook her head.

Katharine and I had never been an actual couple, but we shared a mutual distaste for the same things: corporate ambition, fast food, oversized cars, reality TV, politics, and optimistic people. We tended to find each other at just the right moments—when we both needed someone to justify our misery.

The two dairy cows I was supposed to keep track of had gone rogue. I'd milked them in the barn, and when I was leading them back to their pen, they trotted off. Katharine had witnessed the entire episode. At the time, she stood in the middle of the gravel driveway wearing her signature outfit: a purple-and-gray flannel and sweatpants. She sipped coffee. The autumn sun felt like a quilt. When I managed to lose the cows, she told me I was worthless. A few seconds later she clarified: "A worthless farmer."

"Since when did you start explaining yourself?" I said.

"Vincent," she said. She stepped toward me, set a delicate hand on my face. "I hope you don't love me, sweetheart."

"Why would I?" I said. "When have I ever?"

●　　●　　●

The dairy cows stood at the edge of the driveway, thirty-some feet away, gnawing on tufts of grass. Katharine continued to lean against the wooden fence with a piece of grass in her mouth like it was the most natural thing. I jogged around, swung wide, hoping to flank from the rear and herd the cows back. I got close, but they just hopped off the gravel and into the dull-green pasture that wasn't meant for their grazing. Started chewing on more grass.

"C'mon you motherfuckers," I said. Frustration rose up through my chest. I stuck my hand in my pocket and pulled out the shiny brown buckeye Katharine had given to me as a gift last fall. I meant to return the favor but never got around to it. I pressed into the groove, just big enough for my thumb. The cows gawked at me with those velvety dark eyes. They didn't have names. Lyle's wife, Leslie, referred to them as Number Eleven and Number Twelve—those classic looking dairy cows with patches of black and white and the tail that whips back and forth. Leslie took excellent care of the cows—raised them on good grass—and their coats shined in the morning sun.

"Here we go, girls," I said. I made a clicking sound with my mouth similar to how Leslie called them. Didn't work. I sprinted in their direction with hope to scare them back. Didn't work. I sparked firecrackers I'd found in Lyle's junk drawer—tossed them in the grass behind the cows. Katharine held her hands over her ears. Pop-pop-pop. The cows scampered away, but in the wrong direction—hauling ass toward the Catholic Church that sat on the black-top road two miles away. Lyle's driveway was two miles long with nothing in between. That church was the closest thing to the farm. Otherwise it was just limestone bluffs and steep ravines. This was the Driftless region of northeast Iowa. The land looks alarmingly different than the rest of the state, which isn't possessed by dramatic hills and valleys. Millions of years ago the glacial drifts settled and leveled most of the Midwest flat as a concrete slab but spared this region and left it full of mysteries.

I'd started knitting two months prior to this at the recommendation of Katharine, who said it would calm my nerves while I tried to stay sober and contemplate ways of getting my wife and kids back. At home in my apartment, I'd knit with earplugs in so I wouldn't have to hear people yelling in the halls or screwing next door. Knitting wasn't so bad. I planned on making my kids' Christmas presents—hats, blankets—basic stuff.

"What should I do?" I said to Katharine. Her dark hair was cut short so it showed her neckline.

"Come sit by me." She sat down, crossed her legs. She unraveled a plastic grocery bag that held our knitting supplies. She handed me the blanket I was working on. It was her answer to almost everything.

●　　●　　●

There are things about our time here that I'll never understand. Technology, for one. Fucking with food supplies, for another. All those chemicals and made-up ingredients destroying our physical and mental health so corporations can make ungodly profits and cloak it under the veil of feeding the world. Lyle taught me all that. And I think he's right. I lost my mother, dead at age fifty-four, and I'll never understand that either. She'd been sober for ten years. A healthy person. Smiled a lot. Cared for people. Cancer consumed her spinal cord, her brain. Died in a hospital bed. I never knew her like

I wanted.

I've dreamt of her every six weeks since she's been gone. In the dreams, I hug her like she's still alive, and then I wake up and cry all day. I tell myself I'm a grown-ass man, that I shouldn't be sobbing like that. But I miss her. She hardly knew my kids.

The first dream I had, she was there in the dining-room. I said to her, "Mom, where have you been? I've been looking all over for you." She didn't reply, just smiled. I looked behind me in the kitchen where all my family stood, and I said, "You guys, there she is, she's right there." They all gave me that look that people have been giving me since I was in middle school, like I don't know what the fuck I'm talking about, and then I turned around to prove she was there, and she was, but right away, she started shrinking. I stood up from the dining room chair. "Mom," I said. "Don't do that, Mom." I stood over her, looking down, pleading with her: "Don't do that." But then she was gone. I woke up after that, agitated. All day, it was like being hung over, only worse. My eyes were practically swollen shut, like a ten-round prize fighter. All day long, my shoulders would shake up and down, and I'd squeeze out tears between my swollen eyes.

At the time, Katharine was the only one in the world I trusted with this. She never betrayed me or what I shared about my mother. And a person who sits and listens to you— I mean really listens—is there anything in this world more valuable?

"Don't rush through it," Katharine told me about my dreams, my mother. I was standing next her, watching the cows. Our knitting supplies lay in clumps at our feet. Katharine rolled a joint on top of the fence post, smoked some, and passed it. I took a small amount and passed it back.

"Your kids doing well?" she said.

"I've got them next weekend." I reached into my pocket for the buckeye and held it in my hand, rubbed it. "They're getting big, you know, sassy and shit."

"What're you reading these days, Vincent?" It was the kind of question only Katharine would ask.

"*Knitting for Dummies*," I said. She managed a chuckle. I wanted to tell her about the books I'd been reading about building a yurt, but for now, I was gonna keep that to myself. Every time I shared one of my dreams, they'd seem to instantly dissolve.

We stood there for a while, not saying anything. Katharine slipped into one of those satisfying stares. I looked around us—the bluffs and trees and pasture that barricaded the land. I refocused on Katharine, who squinted into the horizon, eyelashes meshed together.

"This is the freshest air in the world," I said.

"Nothing prettier than this," she said.

● ● ●

I could see the cows standing in the driveway, like art models, or statues. I held a newly knitted blanket in my hand, up against a fall-blue sky. One side appeared longer than the other.

"Your work is good," Katharine said.

I leaned in, and she let me kiss her on the mouth. But she was somewhere else.

I set the blanket down and drank some of the raw milk—the stuff I'd milked out of Eleven and Twelve before they cantered away from me. It tasted thick and slightly sour at first, but then it was fine. Tasted like everything else from the store, but a little warm. Lyle suggested I drink the milk. He said there were enzymes in raw milk that aren't in store bought. "Gets eliminated with pasteurization," he said. I set the milk down and dug the buckeye out of my pocket, rolled it around my palm. Katharine took a sip of the milk and made no motion whether she liked it or not.

● ● ●

Mid-afternoon, Katharine and I strolled around to the back-side of the barn, just for something to do. Asian beetles and box-elder bugs swarmed the doorways and window sills, and the air smelled of decaying leaves. Katharine folded her arms in front of her, looked down at her shoes.

"Vincent," she said. "I have a decision to make." She placed her left hand over her navel. A lone, wispy cloud angled its way across the northern sky.

"Wait," I said. "You're—"

"Yes," she said.

I looked at her stomach, which gave no indication. The world temporarily fogged over. I went to her, held her.

"I can drive you anywhere you need to go," I said.

"I don't need your advice," she said.

"I would never—"

"I know what you meant," she said.

"Does he know?"

"Most likely not."

"Is it his?"

"God you're an asshole," she said. She turned away from me. This new information suddenly changed everything about the last eighteen hours we'd been together.

"We're gonna be okay," I said.

"Don't say 'we'," she said.

"I'm trying to help," I said.

"Help by not saying anything," she said.

I kissed her temple, her forehead. She felt cold. She had nothing to give. She needed her own time to figure things out. Katharine pulled away from me, slouched over to the barn, head down, arms folded. She looked small, and I wanted to protect her.

But maybe that's not how I *really* felt. Maybe I wanted her insomuch as she needed me—for her to ask of me, to rely on me, to depend on our being together. The truth is, neither of us knew what we wanted anymore, and up until then, I always felt as if she had my best interests in mind. But now she had other concerns. I know now that she wanted some kind of permission from me to keep it. For me to show any amount of surprised joy. But that moment is gone.

I refocused on the cows.

On the gravel driveway, I spotted them still grazing nearby, near a toolshed. "Hi sweeties," I said, waving to them. "Just want you to know I'm still here." I stood there and took in the sights. Lyle's mutts found me, and their tails slapped my jeans. I petted them both. They sat down. It was that time of day, mid-afternoon, when everything's quiet. Even the birds had stopped singing. They just fluttered around from evergreen to evergreen, silent as an empty confessional. The apartment was never like this. People milling around outside at all hours of the day, begging and screaming for someone or something.

I found a lawn chair and sat down. I rubbed my temples, thought about Katharine's baby—a little creature I would never meet. I thought about my own kids, how well they would like it out here, chasing the mutts and running around the pasture with the cows. I also thought of my ex-wife. I looked at the trees that lined the ravine, day dreaming an entire conversation with her—thinking about what I might say if I ever got a third chance at things. The gray-brown branches of the trees below started to form into shapes. They lifted together in the wind, and I watched Lyle's grass-grazing cattle herd—the ones he'd eventually butcher—work their way up the ravine. Lyle assured me that grass-grazing cattle could change the world. "Swap out grain for grass, Vincent," he'd said. "You know how much carbon we could harness in the roots of that grass? How much cleaner our water would be?

How much healthier our meat would be?" I was never good with these kinds of questions, but his confidence made me feel like there might be something better out there.

●   ●   ●

The dairy cows slipped away without my noticing. They were nowhere to be seen. They say animals move toward food, but they're also prone to take the easiest path. It made sense to me that I should try walking the gravel driveway. It wasn't loose gravel. It was packed-down and easy to navigate.

I sauntered down the driveway, calling for the cows. I turned back to see about Katharine, but she must've been huddling inside, collecting herself. The mutts joined up and quartered in front of me, working the edge of the driveway, sniffing at everything. I walked at a good clip, working up a sweat. The land, shades of autumn, stretched and rolled out like a wrinkled sheet. I peered into the ravine, thinking Eleven and Twelve might be grazing below, or drinking water from the creek. They weren't.

Near the end of the driveway, when I emerged from around the bend, under a canopy of bare tree limbs, I spotted gray-haired couples stepping out of Buicks and Oldsmobiles, wearing jeans and light fall jackets. I stood next to where the driveway and the parking lot of the church intersected and watched all those senior citizens going to Saturday evening service. Seeing them at that moment filled me with something close to hope. I waved, flapping my hand back and forth. Some waved back. They moved like snails, slow-stepping over the gravel parking lot. I could've hugged every one of them, given them a little pat on the ass. I loved them all.

Turkey vultures soared above the trees. I shoved a hand in my pocket and found my buckeye. I rubbed it vigorously. More cars and trucks pulled in. This was a country church, no houses nearby. Just an open grass field that butted up against

a stretch of woods. An old, beat-up basketball hoop was connected to a shed behind the church, but there was no concrete
to dribble on, just rocks and weeds.

Other vehicles pulled in and parked at the edge of the lot
where the grass and gravel came together. I waved at more
folks and tried to look friendly. There were some young couples holding hands, strolling toward the church. Still, it was
mostly elderly couples, slightly slumped over. I heard something scuff the gravel behind me. Katharine was there, about
twenty feet away, looking small and frail against the back-
drop of hundred-year-old oak trees, a few rust-colored leaves
still clinging to their crooked branches. I held my hand out
for her to take, and she did. She rested her head against me,
and then I put my arm around her and brought her in closer.
She smelled like someone who'd been walking into the wind,
with a hint of lavender.

A minivan rolled up, and a family hopped out. Mom
and Dad and two boys wearing jeans and flannels. I let go of
Katharine. The last boy out forgot to close the sliding door. I
walked over. They noticed me right away.

"We're just farm-sitting down the driveway, here," I said,
pointing in that direction. "We were just out for a stroll. You
left your door open."

"How's that going for you?" the man said.

"What's that?" I said.

"The farm-sitting," he said. He walked around the van
and slid the door shut.

"We're missing the milk cows, but I have an idea they
might come back by morning so I can pump out all that
milk." Lyle said if their teats engorge it can be painful as hell.
I grabbed my chest, said to the stranger, "You know how they
engorge." The man looked at his wife and kids then back at
me. He kind of chuckled. Then they started for the church.

I wasn't ready to let them go. I looked back at Katharine,
but she was paying attention to something off in the distance.

Her hands were folded out front, the mutts sat at her side. The lowlight softened her face. She looked young and sad and helpless. Beautiful, really. Maybe the most beautiful I've ever met. I turned back to the family strolling away from me.

"I've got two kids," I said. The family stopped, glanced back. "I'm a good enough dad, just not a good farmer." Some people at the church entrance halted and looked at us. I didn't know what else to say.

The man—long-limbed and tall, but not skinny—pulled off his hat, which said, *Allamakee County Co-op*. He patted the top of his head. His jeans were dark blue. The woman wore a fitted canvas coat that hung to mid-thigh with a tie around the waist. The man took a step closer to me. I thought he might be inspecting my hair, which was shaggier than usual, growing over my ears. "Well," he said, "church starts here in just a few minutes, so we better keep moving. You're both more than welcome to join us."

"Oh, thanks," I said. "I think we'll just make our way back. We've got dinner waiting on the counter," I lied. I stuck my hands in my back pockets and realized that I'd brought along both knitting needles. I pulled my hands out and rested them at my sides.

"You'll need to go looking for those milk cows, you hear me?" he said. "They won't come back on their own."

"Man, we're new at all of this," I said.

"You'll be fine," he said. "Just keep looking—they usually don't wander too far."

"I don't know," I said. I wanted him to help us. I wanted him to relay some instruction, some sure-fire way to get them back.

"All right, then," he said. "Good luck." He waved and turned his back and strolled off to catch up with his family.

When the parking lot emptied of people, I left Katharine where she was, still staring off at the clear white horizon, and snuck up to the church and put an ear to the tall wooden door.

The organ droned, people sang hymns. I moved to a window and watched the backs of their heads. I imagined their eyes sad and sincere, their mouths moving in funny ways.

Another minivan pulled in. I slipped away from the window and acted nonchalant. I stepped off the wooden stoop and greeted the family. I saluted the kids, which is something I'd never done. They saluted back and smiled, marching to the church, holding hands with their parents.

●　　●　　●

I had a family once. My son looked like those kids at the church—engaged and full of love. We hugged a lot. He smiled. We played catch. We'd fish off the side of a dock with night crawlers four inches long. We never caught anything, but we didn't mind. I told him jokes while my daughter sat in a lawn chair and read a book. She only tolerated me, but I thought we were improving. And my wife, she was always there, doing her own thing. We'd catch each other, eyeing one another, and smirk at our dumb luck, our beautiful family. "We're so lucky," she said. "How'd we get so lucky?" The sun would set happy on those days. We were all trying. But as they say, sometimes trying just isn't enough.

●　　●　　●

Katharine and I stood in the church parking lot and watched the sun nestle itself behind the tree-lined bluffs. We started the two-mile walk home. Darkness settled. A slight chill in the air. The dogs moved in front of us, their paws kicking up gravel. I patted my pocket and felt for the buckeye. I thumbed it while I searched for the cows. I called their names. I made that clicking sound, but it didn't travel far, absorbed into my blind spots. We walked for another minute before Katharine latched onto my elbow. Burrowed in close. It was then that I offered her the buckeye. It lay in the middle of my palm. "For luck," I said. "I know you gave it to me, but you might need it more than myself."

She didn't say anything. Just folded my fingers over it and squeezed my hand.

We hiked off the driveway and into a field, still hollering for the cows. The field was uneven, and we were having a difficult time traversing the tufts of grass and mounds of dirt. It was that time of evening when the western sky turns a clear pale white and everything else casts shotgun blue. The air felt crisp, dry. There was nothing around us, just a rolling field and a far-away tree line, its skinny limbs tall and silhouetted. But off in the distance, an orange glow started to form. It wasn't uncommon to burn leaves or brush this time of year. Maybe it was a barn burning. Or maybe a house. We couldn't have known either way. The blaze stayed shallow, never amounted to much. We trekked toward it anyway, just for something to do, and after a while we could smell the faint odor of smoke. Katharine clutched my arm tighter now, like she'd never let go.

● ● ●

That night, farm-sitting, we hiked together for a long time, Katharine at my side. We'd been walking for so long that if we'd tried to stop, even for a moment, it might've felt strange. You see, we had a rhythm going, and it felt good, necessary. And for a while it felt like we were getting closer to the fire, but after we cut across a few fields trying to find its exact location, we understood finally that it was further away than we had originally thought. I didn't mind walking with Katharine by my side, though, so I didn't say anything. Just kept moving into that deep country darkness. Sometime later—I don't remember at which point in the night—she said something to me that, at the time, didn't seem as important as her holding on to my arm. She said, "It's becoming clear to me, Vincent, that we need a more convincing strategy." We kept walking for a while, and I tried to think of something satisfying to say to her, which ultimately never came to me. But here's the thing: until now, I thought she had been referring to the cows.

TODAY YOU'RE CALLING ME LOU

When I get to my grandmother's assisted housing complex in downtown Cedar Rapids, she's outside waiting for me in a lawn chair—the kind with webbing and rivets. She's smoking a cigarette.

"I thought you quit," I say.

"It's my birthday," she says. She laughs and it sounds like motor oil gurgling around her lungs. She unhooks her cane from the arm rest and uses it to stand. She stuffs a folded newspaper under her arm and shuffles toward the car. With Quaker Oats right across the river, the whole place smells like Captain Crunch.

"What's the plan?" I say.

"You're late," she says, walking away from me.

"Sorry, Grandma."

She turns and glares, and points a shaky hand at me. "You know, let's get this out of the way right now: stop calling me that."

"What?" I say.

"Today you're calling me Lou."

"Fine," I say. "Anything you want. It's your birthday." And it makes sense. All of my uncles and their wives call her Lou. My grandpa, when he was alive, called her Lou. Everyone calls her Lou. Short for Louella.

She takes a few more steps and stops. Smoke billows out of her mouth, and her bifocals slip toward the tip of her nose. "Where's your dad?" she says. "He's supposed to be here."

"Second offense," I say. "Lost his license."

"What a dumbass," she says. "No wonder he doesn't visit anymore. No one visits anymore. Christ. You spend your whole life doing this parenting-thing, and then what? No one comes to visit."

I jam my hands into my jean pockets. "They'll visit soon," I say.

"It's too late," she says. "You know, those boys never respected me anyway."

"How about we not talk about it?"

"See," she says. "Even you—won't listen to a goddamn thing I say."

"Look—"

"—you're all a bunch of assholes," she says.

She ambles closer to her former car, which is now mine: a burgundy-colored Buick Century. "May 27th," she says. "Me and JFK." She reminds me every year that they share a birthday, but they don't. His was the 29th. "If he were alive, I'd like to give him a squeeze right now," she says. I walk around her, ignoring the comment. The manicured lawn feels spongy under my feet. I open the passenger-side door and signal for her to get in. She makes eye contact. Her eyes are dull, and her skin looks like lutefisk—wrinkled, weak, translucent. She's wearing jeans with an elastic waist. They look like capris but I doubt that's the original design. She's also wearing a long-sleeve, button-down shirt with a flower pattern. Her gray hair is cut short.

"Are you okay?" I say. "You don't look well."

"I'm fine," she says. "I'm great. I took an extra pill this morning. Nurse says it lubricates the joints." She rubs her elbows. "I feel like a fucking ninja," she says. She ducks under my arm and sits down. "Thanks for holding the door," she says. "You're a gentleman." She flicks her cigarette butt on the ground, next to my Timberland work boots. "Maybe you'll be better than your bastard uncles."

Bastard uncles, I think. But I don't comment. Inside the car my grandma doesn't bother buckling. She runs a finger over the newspaper. I start the car.

"Here," she says, pointing to a section of classifieds scribbled over in yellow highlighter.

"Garage sale?" I say. I read the ad: Lightly used furniture, name-brand clothing, Oprah books, high-end kitchen items, camping gear, a kayak. "What exactly are you hoping to get?" I say.

"I've always loved being on the water," she says. "My best times were on a dock or a boat." I flip the paper over and around, looking at the ads, thinking of what I want to say. It's true: our best times as a family were our every-other-year fishing trips to Minnesota. My grandma, tan, and fishing off the dock or off a rowboat. I've never seen her happier than she was when near some water. She'd rub tanning oil all over her arms and legs, then on my sister and me. We all smelled like coconuts.

"So, the kayak?" I say.

"I haven't been garage sale-ing forever," she says. "Besides, it's too nice out to play bingo." The engine makes a rattling sound while we idle in the parking lot. "Why can't you take care of my car?" she says.

"It's got over two hundred thousand on it," I say.

"Fine," she says. "I don't give a shit as long as we can make it."

● ● ●

This is nothing I want to do. But since we'd lived with my grandparents since I was ten, and since I'd spent almost every birthday with her for the last eleven years, my dad guilt-tripped me into spending the afternoon with her.

Plus, I just finished my first year at the community college, and won't be starting with the landscaping crew for another week.

Plus, my dad said her health was bad, awful, declining

rapidly. And I could see he was right.

●　　●　　●

After we've driven a few blocks—past Mercy hospital, the YMCA, and over the railroad tracks and the Fifth Ave. bridge, where the muddy Cedar River flows below—my grandma says, "You got any vodka?" The sky is perfectly clear, a tender blue. I roll down the window. The Captain Crunch smell is still there. Plus dead carp.

"You don't drink," I say.

"I'm celebrating," she says.

"Do you have money?" I say. "You buy, I fly."

"Buy the good shit," she says, thumbing through her purse.

"Thata girl, Lou," I say.

"Kenny'll love this," she says.

"What's he have to do with it?" Kenny's my uncle, her oldest son.

"He's the sucker who got stuck paying my credit card." After another minute she says, "Buy me some Kools, too. I'm out."

"Really?" I say.

"Quitting was the worst mistake of my life," she says. "Next to having kids."

●　　●　　●

After our pit stop, my grandmother and I cruise residential backroads, avoiding traffic and cops, sipping out of red plastic cups. We pass dilapidated houses ravaged by the flood. Streets, worn and potholed. Yards with junk piled high, and chain-link fences with "Beware of Dog" signs. People sit in their yards, on their porches. The streets look gray with dust. We pass a neighborhood bar where men stand outside the door, smoking and talking. It's dark inside the bar, except for the green and red neon beer lights. We continue driving, trying to make our way to the southeast side of town, toward the garage sale. A Styrofoam cooler is propped up in the backseat. Inside the cooler: a five-pound bag of ice, orange and cranberry juice, and two bottles of Ketel One. After we've been driving for a while, she says, "What's with the two bottles?"

"The other's for later," I say. "I'll put it to good use."

"You've always been one of those fuckers, haven't you?"

"What are you talking about?"

"You know," she says.

I step on the gas and she spills on herself.

●　　●　　●

We waste more time driving around, getting drunk, waiting for the garage sale to start. What kind of garage sale starts at 4:00 p.m.? But who cares? I'm starting to enjoy myself. After a few turns the neighborhoods get a little nicer. My grandma sits quietly. I sip my cocktail and think about the finals I took two days ago. My hope is Engineering. But I'm wondering if I have what it takes. My Calc final didn't go so well. I took time off after high school and worked carpentry with my dad. We were both on antidepressants that didn't work as well as we'd hoped. We had arguments. I'm surprised he still calls for favors. In those two years, I forgot about math. But still. The dream is Engineering.

My grandma asks for another drink so I pull under the Interstate-overpass and mix two more. "Lighter on the orange," she says. "I think it's giving me heartburn." She runs a hand over her chest. After a minute she says, "You still dating that floozy?"

I stop pouring. "Gwen?" I say. "I haven't seen her since high school."

"You've never been great with the ladies, have you?"

"New subject," I say.

She chuckles and then starts to cough. She smacks her chest with her free hand. "Christ almighty," she says, catching her breath.

"You gonna make it?"

She looks out the window. I pour more booze. She puffs on a Kool. "Did I ever tell you about the time I got arrested for drunk driving?"

"You were driving in reverse," I say. "Thirty-five miles per hour, and hit a fire hydrant."

She laughs and coughs again. "That was something," she says. She hands me a cigarette, like it's some kind of reward. "Have one with me," she says. I accept, and light up. "The thing no one knows about that night," she says, "is that it was the last great night your grandfather and I had."

"Oh, yeah?" I say, concentrating on my cigarette and cocktail.

"When he bailed me out of the station...God," she says. "He was so angry, cussing me out in front of the cop. It was so bad that the cop asked if I wanted to leave with him." She takes a drag. "Anyhow, I told the cop I was okay, and when we got outside under the streetlights something happened and your grandfather just started laughing about the whole thing. Then he took me up to Winifred's on First Avenue and we drank and ate a late dinner." She pauses and looks down at her shirt. "I'm drunk," she says. She rests her head on the window. Graffiti under the bridge says: *All y'all motherfuckers, can go fuck yourselves.*

"That's really great," I say. "About Winifred's."

My grandma sits up, rolls her window down. "But all in all he was an asshole," she says. "I should've left him, you know." She sips her plastic cup and looks away from me. "I know how you felt about him. He had all the patience in the world for you and your sister—making birdhouses and shooting that damn BB gun in the basement. But he had no patience for me."

I consider saying something, reminding her of all the fishing trips to Minnesota, all the fish we caught—my grandpa cleaning and filleting, my grandma cooking. They were a team. But the more I think about it, the more I remember how little they were actually together. My grandmother would be in the water or on the dock, sunbathing, or inside the cabin making everyone sandwiches. And my grandpa and I were in the boat: trolling, casting, pulling in fish.

I keep my hands on the wheel, plastic cup between my legs, and focus ahead. I flick my cigarette out the window and start driving. A gust of wind kicks up dirt. A plastic grocery bag kites by.

"Your grandfather," she says, shaking her head. Then she looks at me: "People tell you to never give up," she says. "But I say a person needs to learn when to call it quits. Sometimes you just need to call it done."

We pull up to the curb and park next to the garage sale, but it's not four o'clock yet. Outside, people are strolling on sidewalks or sitting on concrete stoops. The houses in the neighborhood are a lot like my grandparents' former house: modestly sized, ranch-style homes with the concrete steps, handrail, and attached garages or carports. The garages are the families with money. My grandparents always talked about building one, but they never got around to it.

"See that, over there," my grandma says. "I want you to run out and grab it for me." She slurs and fumbles over words, pointing at the green numbers on the radio. "It's four," she says.

"Grandma," I say. "A kayak?"

"I told you not to call me that, it sounds stupid. And, yes, the kayak. I have plans to be on the water."

"It'll probably cost a fortune."

"We'll Jew'em down," she says.

"Lou," I say. "You can't say shit like that anymore."

She pushes my shoulder. "Go!"

I speed walk past a big woman wearing one of those purse-backpacks. We bump elbows.

"Watch it," she says.

"Sorry," I say.

I stand next to the kayak. It's red and black, and standing on end beside the garage door, where a man with a mustache sits in a brown folding chair. He's behind a square card table, emptying rolls of change into a metal box with money dividers. "I'll take this," I say.

"Great," he says. "I thought it would go fast."

The big woman approaches. "I was here first," she says. She's out of breath.

"I think I was here first," I say, and then look at the guy with the mustache. He stands.

"I see what you're saying," he says to the woman. He's a soft-spoken guy with dainty hands. He's wearing Birkenstocks and khaki pants that are rolled up to mid-calf. The big woman brings her doughy arm through the backpack loop and takes out a checkbook. She's wearing an oversized shirt and tights that show the dimples in her legs. Her face is round and her eyes scrunch together.

My grandma shuffles up. She's got orange juice and cranberry stains on her flowered shirt. She holds her drink and cigarette in one hand, and uses the other to balance on the card table. Her eyes narrow on the big woman.

"Just relax," I say, preemptively. Then: "Where's your cane, Lou?"

"You couldn't fit into that goddamn thing anyway," she says to the woman.

The guy with the mustache puts a prissy hand over his mouth. "Now, now," he says.

"It's for my son," the woman says, looking at me and the guy with the mustache.

"She was *parked* here first," the guy with the mustache says.

"So she could technically say that about any of these items," I say. "She could say that about"—I point to a deep fryer inside the garage—"anything."

"I want that, too," she says.

"Good God, you fat bitch," my grandma says.

"Jesus, Lou," I say. "Go wait in the car."

"Who is this woman?" the big woman says to me.

"I'm his grandmother," Lou says. "I'm in assisted living, for Chrissake. Is this too much to ask? You take the fryer, I'll take the canoe." She gives the big woman a long, hard stare and sets her drink on the table. She takes a drag.

"It's actually a kayak," Mustache says.

"You know what the hell I'm talking about," Lou says. Mustache sits back down, and the big woman shakes her head, lets out a sigh of disgust, and walks to the fryer.

"You learn quick, you overweight piece of—"

I shove my hand over her mouth.

"Get her out of here," the big woman yells.

"She's drunk," I say. "I'm really sorry."

I take my grandma's arm and pull her back to the car. She can barely stand, let alone walk. We weave between people who are pretending to peruse tables. I nod and smile at them. When we get to the car I open the door.

"Thank you," my grandma says. "You're still a gentleman."

"What the fuck?" I say.

"I don't want to hear it," she says. Her eyes close, her head sways. This is the kind of thing that reminds me of all that went wrong in my childhood. My grandma: yelling at people in the grocery store; hitting on my teacher at parent-teacher conferences; arguing with people at Walmart, trying to get a better deal on some already discounted silverware.

I wait until we've made eye contact and tell her: "Wait. Here."

When I walk back to gather the kayak and supplies, I see a young man sitting in the big woman's minivan. Earbuds plugged into his ears. He mouths the words to some song. He's also overweight, cheeks large and pink. When I walk past, he looks at me and nods. I nod back.

"The kayak was going to be for him," the big woman says to me, as she's hauling the fryer from the garage to her minivan.

"Well, he doesn't look old enough anyway."

She gives me a look, and I now realize that it must seem ridiculous that my grandma wants this kayak.

"Your grandmother's an evil woman," she says.

"I'm really sorry about that," I say. "Let me help you." The fryer is heavier than I thought, but we load it, and she gives me a sympathetic stare.

"Good luck," she says, nodding toward my grandma.

I also apologize to the man with the mustache. He's kind and sympathetic. Even so, he won't accept less than fifty for his kayak. I only have twenty, so I barter away the unopened bottle of Ketel One and a book of CDs.

"This feels a bit excessive," I say, as I'm digging out the Ketel One from the cooler. He's standing next to me.

"Hey," he says. "You agreed."

My grandmother's nodded off in the front seat and I notice she's wet herself. Mustache helps me mount the kayak onto the car. He's giving me the straps, paddle, and a life vest that'll probably never get used.

I disassemble the paddle, throw the life vest in the back, thank him, and start the car. Grandma wakes up. She looks down at herself. "It's a helluva thing," she says. I touch her shoulder and ask if she's okay.

"It's a helluva thing," she says, again. She won't look at

me, but even from the side I can tell that her eyes are sad and watery. Her hands rest in her lap, shaking. I rub her shoulder, then her arm.

"It's okay, Lou," I say. "It happens."

●　　●　　●

She insists on visiting the Coralville Reservoir, which is twenty miles south of Cedar Rapids, near Iowa City. She wants to be on the water, and if we time it well, we should have an hour of sunlight.

The blacktop roads are smooth. It's a quiet ride. I look out at the newly planted corn and bean fields, little sprouts, ankle high. A hawk hovers over the ditch, dives into the grass. The leaves are just starting to pop and they're a soft, vulnerable green. I wonder if this is what she wanted for her birthday.

At one point, I think Lou is passed out. But when I reach to turn on the radio, she asks if I still have the quarters. She says, "We're gonna get you to college with those bicentennial quarters. Must be a couple hundred dollars there. You still have them, don't you?"

"I'm in college right now," I say. The quarters were her idea. We were supposed to save every bicentennial quarter and fifty cent piece by putting them away in old vitamin C containers. I'm not sure why she chose those particular coins, but that's what she did. When I graduated from high school, she gave me the containers. I'd never seen her so happy. She said, "We're gonna get you to a university, aren't we?" I don't have the heart to tell her, but I spent the whole wallop of cash—$225—the summer after I graduated, on a glass pipe, an ounce of cannabis, and three cases of St. Ides malt liquor.

"I'm not talking about a community college," she says. "I'm talking about a university. Promise me you'll finish at a university. I worked hard to save that change."

"I promise," I say. "It's part of the plan."

"I thought I'd live long enough to see at least one of my kids or grandkids graduate from college," she says. "And that won't be the case." She shakes her head.

"I'm gonna go," I say. "I promise."

●   ●   ●

The reservoir's quiet. I unload the kayak and set it on the beach. The sun hovers above the treetops and the sky is showing violet. The air is damp and fresh. Behind us, walkers and bikers travel the path that runs beside the bank. The water looks like a bowl of black bean soup. "So, are you just planning to take it out for a spin?" I say.

"I've never done this," she says. She looks over the water. She closes her eyes and takes a deep breath. A few fishing boats troll along the far shoreline. On our left, two ducks float out across the water.

"Maybe I should try first," I say. I pull the kayak over the sand, closer to the water.

Without turning, she says, "I never knew my father." I look at her, surprised. She continues to stare straight ahead. The water seems to be drawing something out of her. "It's been tough on me," she says. "You wouldn't know this, of course, because no one really knows about it, not even your dad or your uncles."

I kick off my boots and bury my feet in the cold sand. She seems sober. "Smoke?" I say, and hold out the pack of Kools. She takes one.

"My mother," she says, "got knocked up by some guy with the last name Burke. That's my maiden name. I don't know why, it's not a name I know. My mother didn't even take that name. She brought me back to the family farm to get raised by her parents and my aunts and cousins. And she went back to the city and after a few years got married to the person she nannied for, this guy with four kids of his own. They were all bratty little shits. I went to live with them, but that didn't go over too well." She shakes her head. "So I went back to the farm and never really talked to her, my mom. But it's the part about my father—" She looks at me now, her eyes bright and watery. "Never knew him," she says. "Never even saw a picture." She throws her cane into the reeds and pulls off her shoes. She wades into the water, her arms out for balance. Before I can comment, she says, "Help steady the kayak." I hold out the life vest, but she shakes her head. "Light me up one more of those." She points to the pack lying on the grass at the edge of the sand and water. "And hand me what's left of that bottle."

The water comes up to her thighs. She's fully clothed, and wearing a visor, now, even though it's dusk. It's pulled down to just above her eyes, so whenever she looks at me she has to cock her head back. "Help me in," she says.

As she climbs in, it wobbles, and I have to hold it steady while she gets her balance back. Her hands shake and her shoulders bunch up around her neck, as if she's cold. But I let go anyway. The bottle of vodka sits between her legs. A cigarette dangles from her mouth. She paddles. "I have no idea what I'm doing," she says. "But I'm a fast learner."

"You look great, Lou," I say. She's smiling. She stops paddling. She looks in the direction of the early evening sun.

"About my father," she says. "I just needed to tell someone about that."

"It's fine, Lou," I say. "Really, it's just fine."

"You're a gentleman," she says. And then she turns away and skims the paddle over the surface. It takes her a minute to find center. But eventually she does, and she looks comfortable. Short strokes propel her forward. And for a while, I simply watch. She yells a few things, but none of it makes sense. I imagine she's in some kind of daze.

I look behind me and no one is around. Bats flutter overhead and the sky's fading into a plum color. I think about yelling out to her—she's drifted pretty far—but it's almost too silent, and feels wrong to interrupt something so peaceful. Even so.

"Grandma," I yell. But she doesn't look in my direction. "Lou!"

I sit on the beach and continue to watch her. The sand is cool and coarse. I cup some, and it runs like a waterfall between my fingers. I lie on my back. I close my eyes and make a mental note that at some point—maybe tomorrow or the next day—I need to buy air fresheners to get rid of the cigarette smoke in the car. Then I'll check my final grades. Around me, some college kids have filtered onto the beach. One guy is flying a kite. How long have they been here? I try to imagine what this looks like to them: old lady in a kayak.

"Lou," I say. "Come on back and let me try." People look at me, but I don't care. I'm still pretty drunk, and she's getting out there a ways. I stand and wade into the water. I try not to panic. Some guy in a Hawkeyes hat comes by.

"Everything okay?" he says.

"She's experienced," I say. "She knows what she's doing."

And while I'm talking to this guy, she actually starts paddling directly away from me, toward a cove on the other side of the reservoir. The guy's holding a can of beer wrapped in a koozie. He's a well-built kid who seems genuinely worried. "What should we do?" he says. "It's almost dark."

"Like I said," I say. "She knows what she's doing."

The college kids scatter. Once again, I'm sitting on the beach, waiting. I rub my eyes and squint toward the darkness. Over and over, waves break on the shore. In the distance, I can hear something—maybe the slap of a paddle. I stare, hoping my eyes will adjust, but they don't. And whatever I've heard eventually fades, moving out and away on the water.

LIE
HERE
NEXT
TO ME

Sally sat on the toilet longer than needed. She liked the view out the bathroom window— the overgrown bushes and black raspberry canes, and several unidentifiable saplings that were growing through the mess of bramble. A catbird lighted on the bronze nob atop the unused flagpole that sat off to the side of the brush. The bird made a squeaky flamboyant pitch. Sally scrunched up three plies of toilet paper and dabbed herself dry. She set the lid down, paused, then put it back up. She thought, what's the point? It was only her and her bedridden mother who, with Sally's assistance, got up once a day to pee. Her mother was forty-six. Sally stared inside the bowl before looking back out the window. Sometimes, for reasons that were unclear to her, she inspected the toilet water after she went to the bathroom. It was a new thing, a new habit. She had a lot of new habits.

She paced into the living room and unplugged the answering machine and silenced the telephone. She was tired of the calls; tired of the check-ins from friends and family; from her grandmother; tired of the "how is she?" and "how are you?" and all the well-meaning but annoying people who had *no fucking clue*.

Out of habit, because it was a Friday, she decided to bake a cake. She was nineteen, back from her first year at the University of Wisconsin-Madison. She'd been wearing the same outfit for the last four days: underwear and a t-shirt that read, "Ultimate World Champions"—a gift from her ex, Monica, who was currently playing on UW-Madison's nationally ranked Women's Ultimate Frisbee team. They'd split up earlier in May on "mutual terms." But not really so mutual. Monica was a senior, just graduating, and thought it only fair to herself, and Sally, that she start the "real world" without consideration for anyone or anything but her future, her career, her whatever. Sally had told her that she understood, mostly. Now, she checked her phone, which was also on silent. She read a new text from Monica. This year's tournament had started two days ago. Defending champions. Apparently, according to the text, they were, yet again, in the championship game. And oh, *I miss you*!!! Sally sniffed the air around her, aware of how greasy her hair and skin looked and felt; aware of the odor coming from her hard-to-reach and easy-to-reach places. She ran her tongue over her teeth and could feel the grime that had collected there. She felt, in a word, disgusting. But aside from the actual time commitment, cleaning oneself would mean an effort and energy that she simply could not muster. She thought of replying to Monica, but why? To say, *Good luck! Go get em tiger!* To say, *Fuck off don't ever text me again!* To say, *My mother is dying*, and: *I miss you too*. Sally set her phone down. She decided on none of the above. She was good at multiple choice tests and knew when to choose "D." The championships were being played in Boulder, Colorado, and Sally knew it was going to be a drunken pot fest, and she knew Monica would be having the time of her life, one last hoorah with the Ultimate team. Sally tried to convince herself not to care. *The bitch wanted to break it off*. But the thought of Monica with others was too much. She took one big breath, tried to compose herself, and resolved to leave her phone in a drawer.

Sally gathered a bowl and a hand mixer. She rifled through the pantry for a cake mix, but there was none to be found, which was odd. She climbed onto a stool and searched the top and far reaches of the cupboards above the stove, the fridge, and the ones near the sink. What she found instead was a small bag of shake and a one-hitter. She'd forgotten about them until that moment. She pulled the one-hitter out and threw the bag away, not because she didn't want the pot. She did. But rather, she assumed, like most things that sit for too long in a cupboard, that it had gone bad.

Sally put some ingredients into a bowl: oil, eggs, sugar. She looked at it for a while. She went to the living room and turned on the television. It had been weeks since she watched television. It made her dizzy. All the commercials and glamour and glitz, she could feel her stomach tighten every time she watched, but this time, instead of watching, she simply turned it on and left. She thought the noise in the house might help, might somehow slow the process of things growing stale, and offer some passive interaction. This, after all, is all she ever wanted. Direct interaction—with friends or whomever—was tiring. Exhausting, really. She preferred her interactions on the periphery, with the ability to dip in and out when necessary. She'd rather be an observer, a listener, of a conversation between two strangers than have to maintain one of her own, even with someone she knew well. She could interact with the television as much or as little as she liked, and still, it was almost too much.

She tiptoed down the hallway to the last room on the right. Her mother was underneath a comforter, sleeping, barely breathing, really, and Sally wondered how long it might be? She wasn't into prolonging the inevitable, like her relationship with Monica, and understood when things needed to be over. She remembered her dog, a dog that had been with her parents long before Sally was born. To compare her mother to her childhood dog was an insensitive line of thinking, she knew, but she went with it anyway. It was some rescue mutt that had lived far longer than anyone had expected. Toward the end of its life it had seizures and blindness, and it was living, Sally understood even at the age of six, in a bad way. Still, her parents grieved the end of its life as if it were some huge surprise. Even then, Sally knew the ultimate outcome. "Why cry?" she asked her mother. "Isn't she in doggy heaven?" And her mother's reply, Sally concluded, didn't make any sense. "We cry," her mother said, "because we shouldn't ignore our urges."

Sally's urge, now, which she hated, was to cover her mother's face with a pillow. Not because she didn't love her. She did very much. But because it would speed up an altogether painful process. Speeding up one's death wasn't a new argument, but now that she had to face the issue head on, it felt urgent. It felt necessary. She understood, and, in a way, despised herself for thinking such things about anyone, let alone her mother. "Can I bring you anything?" she said.

Her mother shook her head, eyes closed. A permanent grimace on her face. Sally opened a window. Outside the sun was bright and the air felt fresh. One of those spring days that everyone in the Midwest lives for; those days with a cool breeze and clear, but not overwhelming, sky. Sally picked up one of the pillows, fluffed it, and lay down next to her mother. If her father were still around—he, himself, gone, whereabouts unknown—maybe he would've put a comic twist on the plight of a woman who had been "healthy" most of her life. The irony was lost on everyone in her extended family, a family whose humor wasn't prone toward the cruel ways of the world. In a way, there was something even precious about this slow-down moment of her life, this time-warp, these moments when all she had to focus on was her mother. It was like this for her: her thoughts pulling her one way, and then another, simultaneously tender and hideous. Sally wondered about her own time—how would it happen? Who would be there? Anyone? Unlike her extended family, she didn't talk about death, but wasn't scared of it either. Death was simply part of what happens. Nothing more, nothing less. Did anything happen thereafter? She wasn't opposed to the idea; in fact, she liked the idea in a way, but had come to the conclusion that thinking about the unknown was pointless. And that was okay with her. The one part that tripped her up: thinking about her own mother drifting alone into what Sally thought of as the black nothingness.

She took her mother's hand: weak, limp, almost lifeless. Her mother struggled onto her side. She touched Sally's face. "Sweetheart," she said. She ran a finger along Sally's smooth olive skin, her fingernail just barely grazing the surface. These were the moments that took Sally by surprise, the ones that pulled her out of her own mind. It always startled her, the way her mother's presence could unsettle her. "Lie here next to me, sweetheart," her mother said, closing her eyes. Sally started to sob. She buried her face into her mother's chest and neck. Her mother wrapped her free arm around, and held her.

●　　●　　●

Sally peered into the Pyrex. The only thing more fearful than making a bad cake was leaving the house to get a premade mix and seeing all those faux-cheerful faces at the grocery store. So she scavenged the kitchen for ingredients: flour, baking soda, chocolate chips, etc. She found everything she needed. She preheated the oven. She used a Kitchen Aid 5-speed hand mixer and swirled the stuff around. She and her mother used to make a cake every Friday after school and work. It was their thing. Families had their traditions, and this was theirs. They didn't have money to go out to eat, so they stayed in, and while Sally's friends were out at pizza parlors, or burger joints, or some fancy restaurant, her mother had convinced her that this was in fact what every kid wanted, and so this was what they did. Every Friday: no dinner, just cake. Maybe—maybe—her mother's only "unhealthy" thing.

And it was also the one thing that they kept to themselves, their shared secret. But Sally wasn't sure why. Her mother had never said to keep it between them, but something about their Friday cake tradition, Sally felt, even at a young age, would be cheapened if others were to find out. So they never spoke of it, just made it, and shared it, together.

She clicked the mixer off. She could hear her mother's moans, unintelligible mumbles, and Sally dropped the mixer into the bowl and walked down the hallway. The television flashed at her, playing a commercial for a forthcoming DC Comic movie—*Man of Steel* or some such. She helped her mother sit up in bed. She wondered if she'd ever have a chance to tell her, or if it really mattered. She'd dated boys in high school, even slept with a couple of them, but hadn't found the time or space before her mother got sick to tell her about Monica, her first real girlfriend. There'd been others, but no one serious, therefore she hadn't wanted to tell her, though Sally knew her mother would've been more than supportive. Her mother spit up bile into a metal dish. Her stomach convulsions—the ones associated with throwing up—were weak, almost unable to bring up the unwanted. "Water?" Sally said, holding up the glass. "Something else? Juice?" Her mother shook her head, but Sally said, "Open up," and swabbed out her mouth. Her mother opened and closed her lips together like a guppy swimming around an aquarium.

Sally went to the bathroom and ran warm water over a washcloth. She wiped around her mother's neck and arms and face, and afterward she massaged her legs and arms, something she'd seen her mother's friend do the other day. Her mother's friend, a physical therapist, said it was good to keep the blood moving, and this was the way to do it. Sally kneaded her mother's atrophied limbs, and as she worked, she sensed her mother calming. Her breathing grew slow and steady.

●　●　●

Sally checked her phone. She didn't want to. But wanted to. Monica's text said, "We WON!!! Back-to-back!!!"

Sally wanted to reply: "I don't give a fuck." But instead, she wrote: "I'm baking a cake." She put the phone back in the drawer. The television was still on, and it surprised Sally every time she walked by. The volume was on low. A gameshow that she didn't recognize.

She greased the nine-by-thirteen dish and dumped in the batter. The oven had been on, and ready, for quite some time. The kitchen had grown warmer, and Sally considered removing some clothing, but she was already in very little. Her underwear—tattered, old, and stained in the crotch—she should've thrown away a long time ago, maybe years ago. But why? Right now, she was upset at herself for even thinking about it. Who cared? No one would see. And that's how it had been for the last two weeks in the house with her mother, with hardly anyone else around save for the occasional hospice nurse, or her grandmother, or someone from her mother's work who brought over food. Sally sat and stared at the television. She pushed the mute button. It was quiet now, and peaceful. For the last two months of school, as her mother had grown weak and dependent, but still insisted that she finish her finals, all Sally had wanted was to sleep. To not think about it. Which is why she never talked about things with Monica. Not because she didn't want her to know—she did want her to know—but because she didn't want the exposure, the vulnerability. She wanted the support, yes, but didn't want to give reasons for needing that support. Instead, she struggled through those final weeks of her first year while partying with Monica—even after they'd broken up, even with how tired, angry, and guilty she felt—and when she wasn't partying with Monica, she dragged herself to class.

● ● ●

The kitchen timer dinged just a few minutes before the doorbell. Sally glanced at the phone and realized that she'd made a mistake. Had she kept the ringer on, or even the answering machine, maybe someone wouldn't be dropping by. She was angered that she hadn't thought of this, and angered more that there were people who would assume that dropping by was okay.

The door opened before she could get there. "Well," her grandmother said. "Is this what college kids wear these days? It smells good in here."

Sally looked down at herself. "I was baking a cake, and, well, I wasn't expecting company." She paced back to the kitchen and put a fork through the middle of the cake. It came out clean.

"I called to tell you I was coming, but something must've happened to your phone. It kept ringing and ringing, but I knew someone was here. How are you, anyway, sweetheart?" Her grandmother set her purse on the fir floor, gave Sally a gentle hug, and walked down the hallway before waiting for an answer. Sally did not want to see her grandmother and mother together. It was okay for Sally to do this on her own: to grieve; to be miserable; to be selfish; to be whatever. But with someone else, especially her mother's mother, it felt too much. As though her mother's imminent passing was connected to so much more than herself, and, for Sally, it was easier to think of this as an isolated moment, affecting only her. She'd been grieving for so long, and by herself, that having to deal with and grieve with others was simply too much. Sally didn't want her grandmother's comfort because that would mean something like being obligated to reciprocate. And she didn't want to comfort anyone but herself. And her mother.

She put her ear to the door. She could hear her grandmother singing in a small voice that reminded her of her mother's voice. Sally's head dropped. Her arms and legs grew instantly heavy. She felt as if she could sleep forever. It had been like this for the last few weeks: a wave of exhaustion would overwhelm her, and all she could do was cry. Long, blathering sobs that, when finished, left her feeling light and sad instead of heavy and sad. She wanted to cry now but not with her grandmother here, so she limped over to the living room and watched television commercials: breakfast cereals, pharmaceutical drugs, financial companies that wanted to help plan your future. A lump tickled her throat until the tickle turned into a burn, and the burn worked its way from her throat into her nasal passages and started to affect her eyes, so that the next time she blinked, tears formed and fell. She looked at the kitchen counter and noticed the one-hitter sitting there. She chuckled out loud at the thought of her grandmother asking what it was. She left it there, hoping for that moment. Her grandmother came out of the room and down the hallway.

"How can I help?" her grandmother said. Her voice was weak. Her eyes were red and she dabbed them with a tissue. Sally observed that her grandmother was always trying to do something; to keep busy; to keep her mind off the situation. She was her namesake, Sally. They looked nothing alike. Not even when her grandmother was her age. Sally had seen pictures. "There's a lot to clean up."

"The house looks fine," Sally said.

"Needs dusting," she said, running a finger over the top of a picture frame. The picture hung in the hallway: a fall camping trip with extended family. "Vacuuming, too, and there's a lot of trash sitting outside that needs to go somewhere. The trashcan, I suspect."

"I'll take care of it later, after you leave," Sally said. "Don't worry about it."

"I'm not worried, I just want this place looking a little

better for guests."

"Guests?"

"Well—"

"No, people are *not* coming over," Sally said.

"Your mother would like to say 'goodbye' to those she's closest with, just a few friends and family. They call it"—she put a hand on her face—"what do they call it?"

"Some living memorial bullshit," Sally said. "Something like that."

"Language, dear," her grandmother said.

"It's not happening."

"This is not about you."

"Or you," Sally said. "And my mother wouldn't want this anyway."

"It'd be good for people to see her one last time," her grandmother said. "It's important."

Sally stormed out the backdoor in her underwear and t-shirt. She sat down, cross-legged in the grass, and rested her elbows on the inside of her thighs and supported her head with her palms. She closed her eyes. What was it about sharing grief with others that left one feeling raw and exposed? It may have been better grieving alongside a stranger than someone she knew so well, like her grandmother. She needed distance from her, from everyone, but that wasn't going to happen.

Her grandmother followed her out to the lawn. "Dear," she said. "I'm concerned for you, and if you're not going to think about this, I will for you." A gentle breeze rustled the uncut grass. "I'll fix you a room at my house for when you come home from college. Everyone needs a place to return to."

"What? No. I don't want this conversation right now."

"What other options do you have, sweetie? Well, maybe your father, I suppose."

"Oh my God," Sally said. "Now you're not making any

sense."

"You should know something about your father," her grandmother said. "I wanted to wait to tell you this—"

"No," Sally said. "I don't want to hear it."

"Your mother's just as responsible for him leaving as—"

"What is your problem?" Sally slapped the ground, got up, and stormed off to a rusted, rickety swing set that had been there since she was a toddler. She sat on the swing, facing away from the house. The seat hugged her hips, and she wondered, even though she wasn't heavy, if it would hold her.

"Stop acting like this," her grandmother said.

"Like what?"

"Like a selfish little bitch." Her grandmother's tone had changed. She was standing directly behind Sally. Sally wasn't sure if she was supposed to laugh or feel angry, or maybe something else entirely. "It's hard enough for me to tell you this, given your mother's condition, without you acting this way. You need to know: your father left, yes, but when he wanted to come back he was pushed away. Your mother is a wonderful mother to you, but she held to these standards, these principles. And I would say it was to a fault. She was just stubborn, your mother."

"Is," Sally said. "*Is* stubborn."

"She was too proud to forgive anyone who may have wronged her. Your father—"

"I can't do this," Sally said. "Not now, please, just not now."

"You need to understand," her grandmother said. "So you have someone after your mother—"

Sally scrambled to the door. She opened it, and as she stepped inside, she looked back at her grandmother who was ambling in her direction. She could smell the cake, probably cool enough to frost. But she wouldn't do that now, she would wait, so she could eat it alone, or near her mother. Because after all, it was Friday, and she'd heard about her father in the past, but didn't want to hear about him now, not this second anyway, and who could blame her? What she wanted more than anything was to eat some fucking cake. To honor, in some way, her mother's tradition. But maybe "tradition" didn't sound right. Her mother would be dead in less than a week, maybe two, so she wanted to call it something more than it was: a celebration? an honoring? She couldn't think of anything satisfactory, and settled on nothing at all. She grew angrier, and wondered how any of this even mattered. Did it matter that they ate cake together every Friday? Did it make one bit of difference for Sally? For her mother?

Her grandmother stepped through the door, but Sally couldn't be in the same room, the same house. She didn't want to hear what she had to say, and didn't want to defend her position of wanting to be alone.

"People will be here soon, dear," her grandmother said. "So I'd advise putting something on, something nice. I'll take care of the cake and straighten up, okay, dear?" As her grandmother droned on, while busying herself in the kitchen, Sally tuned out. It was easy to do. She'd been tuning out for most of her life, and while it had been a point of contention for her mother, her teachers, her friends, and, at times, Monica, she now felt that it was her greatest asset. She watched out the front window as the mail carrier made his way down the street, sorting and stuffing mail into mailboxes. While this happened, she thought of a time in the future when it would just be her, and no one else. Maybe her grandmother. For a while, anyway. Then she thought of Suzanne Goolsby, the full figured girl from the suburbs of Milwaukee who she'd met a few weeks into the school year, and who, on a night when they were supposed to be studying science for non-majors, kissed Sally from her neck down to her navel before ripping off her pants and underwear. Sally remembered staring at the top of Suzanne's head just before she had an orgasm so intense that she'd flung her head back while sitting in a chair without a headrest, and gave herself what she believed was whiplash.

The mail carrier made his way onto the front stoop. He shoved mail into the mailbox, and it clanked shut. After he strolled out of the front yard, Sally stepped out for the mail and stood there for a moment in her underwear and t-shirt, trying to imagine her way out of this, out of everything: her grandmother, the forthcoming guests. She peered back inside. Her grandmother had cleaned up the baking supplies and was now inspecting the one-hitter. Sally smirked. Her grandmother proceeded to frost and cut the cake into small squares. Sally didn't mind. All she really wanted was one piece to share with her mother. And even more, she wanted to sleep. For days and days, she wanted to sleep the time away. The word that had been rattling around, but she couldn't identify, finally surfaced: weary. Everything was wearisome. Sally knew she needed to take care of herself, but changing and showering, and telling Monica how frustrated she felt would have to come later.

Friends and family members pulled up to the curb and into their driveway, Sally gathered all the energy she could, went back inside, and set the mail down. Without thinking about it, she grabbed the pan of cake, and walked down the hallway.

"Sweetheart," her grandmother said. "People are here now."

Sally went into her mother's room and locked the door. She set the cake on top of the dresser. Then she rummaged through her mother's nightstand until she found a pair of earplugs. Her mother was asleep. Sally heard footsteps in the hallway, then a muted voice and a faint rap on the door.

"Sally, dear?" her grandmother said. "Let's have some cake with our visitors."

Sally looked at the door, the cake. Her grandmother said something else. Sally inserted both earplugs. The world fell silent. She got into bed and rolled onto her side. She set a hand on her mother's hip, nestled closer, and tried to rest.

BETWEEN THE FIREFLIES

In June of 2003, summer after the fifth grade, Alice and I were tasked with taking out the cottontail rabbits that had been devastating her family's vegetable gardens: beans, tomatoes, squash, asparagus, carrots, and more. Alice and her father had put up a five-foot wire mesh fence that kept out the deer successfully, but they hadn't anticipated the small and mid-size rabbits that could fit through the slats with ease and all the heavy damage they could cause. Alice had been my best friend and neighbor for the past two years, ever since she and her family had moved in, and now, less than a week away, her father was deploying to Iraq.

"Take them out," her dad said. "Big ones, small ones, all of them." He looked at Alice, then me. We both stood at attention.

"Roger-that," Alice said.

"10-4," I said.

Alice's father was a taut, slender man who wore gray t-shirts tucked into cargo pants. Alice's parents were active, good-looking people who, according to my mother, had a child before they were ready. They often got confused as her older siblings.

Alice's father led us out back behind the barn to show us the damage done to the crops. The beet-tops had been chewed down to nothing. "Can you believe those cockroaches?" he said in reference to the bunnies. He referred to anyone or anything with whom or which he didn't agree as "cockroaches." For instance: bankers, lawyers, politicians, and corporate types: cockroaches. Rabbits, mosquitoes, humidity, and hoppy beers: cockroaches. "I didn't think in a million years," he said, handing Alice a pellet gun and a slingshot, "that we'd get attacked by something so seemingly harmless. Either one of these should do the trick."

Alice's father marched back to the barn where Alice's mother stood with her arms crossed, waiting for him. He was part of the 322nd Engineering Battalion of northeast Iowa. Alice handed me the slingshot. "I'm not sure about this one," she said. "Seems... *inhumane.*" At the time, I wasn't quite sure what inhumane meant, but I nodded in agreement.

Alice and I discussed matters at her sandbox, which was a tractor tire that lay flat on the ground near the swing set. She cupped a handful of coarse sand and let it slip through her fingers. "Evenings or mornings seem best," she said.

"For what?" I said.

"Killing the bunnies," she said. "They're usually out around those times, don't you think?"

"Are you going to eat them?"

"Disgusting," she said. "Those flea ridden varmints? I'd rather drink my mother's dandelion-nettle tea, which tastes like mud."

"I've never had it."

"Count yourself fortunate."

We—or rather, Alice—devised and drew up a plan in the sandbox using a stick that she had found under the Norwegian maple. The maple had red leaves, but part of the tree was dying off. At one point, Alice's mother had referred to the tree as "anemic."

Alice's plans had me walking along the edge of the tall grass while she lay in wait with the pellet gun. It was a ten-pump, made of real wood, and we'd witnessed her father take out woodchucks and raccoons with it, so it led us to believe that killing a rabbit wouldn't be a problem. We agreed to meet at the end of her driveway every day.

"Why again are we doing this?" I said. "Are we getting

paid?"

"It's not always about money," she said. "You've been brainwashed by corporate advertising and the idea of more, more, more, better, better, better. It's not always about more or better."

"Then what's it about?" I said. I looked at the slingshot.

"Good Lord," she said. "I've gotta go to my dad's assembly."

"The one at the gym?"

"Yeah, it's like a pep-rally or something."

•　•　•

Our first hunting excursion happened at around 6 a.m. several days later. Alice and her mother hadn't ventured outside of their house since the deployment, but the day before our first hunt, I'd lumbered up the road with fresh, warm rhubarb crisp that my mother had made. Alice poked her head out the door. "Tomorrow morning," she'd said. "See you then." And I knew exactly what she was referring to.

The next morning, I jogged to her house holding the slingshot. She was waiting for me at the end of the driveway. Her face was red, puffy. She wouldn't make eye contact. The sun had already been out for an hour but the light was still soft and tolerable.

"Let's work this edge here," she said. It was a bramble that most people would've called "weeds," but Alice's mother and father, even Alice, harvested berries, leaves, and roots from every square inch of their property, so calling it "weeds" wasn't quite right. "Here," she said. "Before you swing around the hedge, let me give you these." She pulled out six ball bearings, each the size of a marble. "You hit a rabbit in the head with this and it'll knock it out cold, and then I can shoot it, or we can smash its head with a rock or log."

"Sounds... inhumane." I smiled, hoping she'd approve of

this word choice.

"Yes," she said. "It does." There was no humor in her voice, and I stared at her for a second too long. "I've never done this before if that's what you're wondering," she said. "I don't want to do this." She clutched the pellet gun, looked at the ground. "But it's not about want, it's about survival."

The land was abounding with rabbits of all sizes: big pregnant mothers, adult fathers, mid-size teens, and even a handful of newborns that for some reason reminded me of water balloons. I tiptoed around the bramble, clutching the slingshot. The birds were loud and flying everywhere: nature's warning.

A rabbit tore out of the bushes and though I couldn't see Alice, I heard her shoot at it while it ran between us. I kept power-walking past the sunflowers, daisies, black eyed Suzanne's, and black raspberry canes. Alice's mother used to host wild edible classes that would attract a lot of people, but this was a small town and once you teach those interested few everything you know, then there's no one left to teach. It becomes, after that, a strategy for convincing others that your way of life is important.

Alice pumped and loaded the pellet gun. We could see each other now, and rabbits were running everywhere. I'd never seen so many: zig-zagging through the dewy grass, leaving little darkened trails behind. When I got to the far end of the property, I turned and came back on the other side of the hedge. Alice stood in the grass with a hand on her hip and the gun at her side.

"How am I supposed to hit a moving target with this?" She lifted the gun. I didn't have an answer, so I kept quiet. As I approached her, something caught our attention and we both peered into the brush, scanned around, and saw a rabbit sitting on its haunches devouring grass and clover. My heartbeat quickened and my breathing grew shallow. Alice set a hand on my shoulder, whispered, "The ball bearings."

We were standing inches apart. I was aware of how close she was. She smelled of lemon, ginger, and peanut butter. She kept a calm hand on my shoulder while I loaded the slingshot. Her breathing was steadier than mine. I brought the slingshot up, and back down, then up again. I think she could sense my hesitation because she stepped back slightly, giving me space to move and breath. I pulled the slingshot back and aimed high because I wanted to miss. I let it rip. The ball bearing hit the rabbit square in the chest. It made a loud unsettling thump, and then the bunny hopped off like it was no big deal. It huddled in the grass, sitting still as a statue. I could've squatted down, reached out, and touched it—that's how close it was. And then, just as I was wondering what to do next, it sort of keeled over on its side, its back legs jerking and twitching, like some wind-up toy, and then it stopped. Alice nudged it with the barrel of her pellet gun. Limp and still and lifeless.

"Internal damage," Alice said. "You must've hit it in the vitals. It takes a moment for that to kick in."

My head dropped. Alice placed her hand on my shoulder again. "It's okay to feel bad," she said. "You *should* feel bad. It means you're human."

"I tried to miss."

"I know," she said. "I saw you adjust your aim at the last second."

I turned to face Alice. "I don't know if I can—"

"Yes, you can," she said. "We've been given a task to complete. Don't be a baby about this, understand, sergeant?"

It was the first time she'd addressed me this way, and it caught me off guard.

She said it again: "I said, do you understand, sergeant?"

"Alice! Phone call!" We both turned. Alice's mother was near the barn waving her over. "Come inside for a moment, hurry!"

She took a hard step toward me. "I need a confirmation

from you, sergeant."

"Roger-that, captain," I said. I put my hand up to salute her.

"Put that down," she said. "You look ridiculous in front of my mom."

"Hurry, Alice!" her mother yelled again.

"And when necessary," she said, "address me as Sergeant-major."

"10-4," I said, though I didn't have any intention of calling her that.

"Now take that rabbit behind the gardens, and meet me back here at dusk."

● ● ●

Dusk in Iowa is a slow process, the sun growing distant and weak, casting long shadows over the open countryside, airborne bugs taking flight from their daytime nests—everything feels calm and steady when the day's demands are tucked away for evening.

Alice was an inch taller than me with knobby knees and sharp elbows, sad eyes and a face that gave the appearance of neediness, though her actions belied such impressions. She had short brown hair and distinct emerald eyes. I felt about her the way I've subsequently felt about most women in my life who I call friends: a profound sense of protection. This, I felt then, was a calling, my deepest need to fulfill. At that point, I think I would've done anything for her, though I doubt she knew any of this. I never actually told her—even in the years since—how I felt.

She strolled down the driveway, pellet gun resting on her shoulder. "I talked to my dad on the phone," she said. "He's leaving tomorrow from California. He called you a marksman. A ringer. A dead-shot."

"Tell him thanks," I said. "When you talk to him again."

"One down, one million to go," Alice said.

Dusk proved worthless. We saw a lot of rabbits, but didn't kill anything. As a way to remind me of the seriousness of our—her—situation, she led me to her father's three asparagus plots. One was well established, one had been planted two years ago, and one he'd just planted a few weeks ago, and this year's crop was skinny, and, well, *anemic* was the word that she used to describe it. Other spears had been chewed down to an inch of the soil. The culprits were still at large.

"If there's no foliage to absorb the sun," Alice said, "then there's no energy being stored in the roots, therefore, they're weak, and next year's crop is bad. Or, worse, nonexistent." Last year, Alice's parents sold bundles of asparagus for five dollars a dozen.

There was just enough daylight left, so Alice set up beer cans on an old maple stump. She held out more ball bearings.

"You're gonna practice," she said. "I want you to shoot them down one at a time." She'd set up a straw bale behind the cans to catch the ball bearings.

I shot once and missed. The impact made a soft, satisfying sound as it hit the straw.

"Again," she said.

And again I missed. "I need to get closer," I said.

"Excuses," she said, "disgust me."

"Let's go inside for some water," I said.

"Only if you can hit one of the cans," she said. "Then we'll go in for lemonade."

●   ●   ●

Alice's mother was a slender woman with a soft smile, and despite the warm temperatures, she wore an oversized sweater. She held up the pitcher and poured us lemonade which had slices of actual lemon in it, different from the Kool-Aid mix that I was used to. Her lemonade tasted more sour than sweet, and had bits of pulp floating at the top. I picked out a green sprig of something from inside my cup. "Leave it in there," she said. "It's mint from the garden."

I removed my fingers and was about to lick the lemonade from the tips, but I thought better of it. Instead, I wiped them off on my shirt.

"How are your parents, Ike?" her mother said. It sounded forced.

"They're good," I said. "My parents ask about you every once in a while."

"Is that right?" her mother said. "What do they ask, dear?"

"How's Alice, mostly."

"How nice," her mother said. "Tell them we're well, won't you?"

Her mother moped around the living room fussing with furniture pillows and other things that seemed fine as they were. I walked to the fridge and looked at a picture of Alice and her parents from a time when they'd first moved in.

"One big happy family," Alice said. She set her glass on the counter before slipping out the front door.

It was completely dark by now, and Alice took my hand and led me out to the field next to their gardens. Fireflies flashed everywhere.

"He's been gone less than two weeks," she said. "But it feels like two years."

"I've never seen so many," I said.

"My mom gets stomach aches from worrying so much."

"He'll be back before you know it," I said. "We'll bomb the shit out of whoever we need to kill and then they'll fly him home."

"You think?"

"I know," I said. Of course, I didn't know anything—nobody at that point knew anything—but it was the thing to say, something to comfort her.

"That sounds awful," she said. "Have you been watching

the news?"

"A little," I said. But nothing on the news made sense to me—the foreign names of people and towns. "I guess it does sound pretty bad. But he'll be fine."

"Promise?"

"Yeah, of course," I said. "Promise."

She smiled and took off her shoes. I did the same. We hopped and skipped around the wet grass with frantic urgency, occasionally bumping into each other and stumbling. When that happened, she laughed. I hadn't seen her smile or laugh in weeks.

That night we caught dozens of fireflies, and we'd watch them in our cupped hands before letting them go. We chased them all over, running and jumping, slipping and falling, following the neon flashes.

"Quick, run, do you see it?" Alice would say. "Now, there. Hurry!" And I'd run beside her, conscious of whose turn it was to catch them.

Above us, a moonless sky. Stars so thick it looked like a smear of vanilla frosting. After we'd worn ourselves out, we sat down and watched as the fireflies continued their nightly conquests.

"They're everywhere," Alice said. We were both out of breath.

"I could stay awake all night," I said.

"Maybe we should," she said.

I grew quiet at the possibility. I wanted to say, yes, but instead we just sat there in silence for a little while longer before she said, "My mom used to sing this song, but I can't remember exactly how it goes. *Life is beautiful like the darkness between the fireflies.*"

"I like that," I said. I set my arm around her in a friendly way.

"But that's not exactly how it goes," she said.

"I like your version," I said.

And she continued singing the wrong words to a beautiful song.

● ● ●

Iraq, Afghanistan. I watched the news almost every night under the erroneous notion that I might see Alice's father, though I never mentioned any of this to her. The news reports were horrible: deaths of innocents; car bombs and suicide bombers; Shiites, Kurds, Sunnis, groups of people I knew nothing about; Terrorists, Al-Qaida, Bin-Laden. And, eventually, Saddam Hussein would be captured. It was a swirl of confusion, as the two wars took place in some alternative universe called the Middle East. The mix of news and political spin was dizzying, and the only thing I heard from my parents were things like: *It's a damn shame.* Or, *when's the nonsense going to end?* My father didn't enjoy talking about these kinds of things. He was a quiet man who blended into the background of my life, so I asked my mother what she thought of it, and she said to me, "Ike, you can't use force where philosophies collide. It was a losing venture from the start." I cringed at the thought. She saw my face and understood. "I know what you're thinking," she said. "Alice's father isn't a bad man. He's doing exactly what he's committed to do. But those who are making the decisions about all of this, well, I guess I don't agree."

● ● ●

The next day was cloudy and overcast with a light drizzle that stayed around most of the day. "This rain is good for hunting," Alice said. "My dad says that animals that take shelter in grass move into open areas, or under branches and bushes, so the grass won't get them too wet. We'll check the woods."

The canopy was in full bloom, and Alice was right. We saw

deer and rabbits huddling underneath low-hanging branches where the rain was kept at bay. She took aim on a mid-size rabbit. I stood next to her, shifting my stance. Alice hesitated. I observed the rabbit's muscles, which tweaked and shook with urgency, poised for flight, but ultimately, an animal will remain stationary if it thinks it can't be seen. When the pellet hit the rabbit, it rose up on its hind legs in slow motion and started pawing at the air, like a cat swatting a fly above its head. Then it came back down on all fours, keeled over on its side, shuddered briefly, and that was that. Alice said she'd never seen anything like it, and I agreed.

"Are you okay?" I said.

"Yeah," she said. "I'm fine. And please, don't ask me that anymore."

"Roger-that," I said, though I couldn't remember another time when I'd asked.

We'd started a small cemetery at the edge of Alice's property. I fetched the shovel and met her there. We buried it, but instead of using crosses made of sticks, we'd chosen a few stones to mark each one. "The rocks," she said, "will be faster and easier than trying to make crosses every time we kill something."

●　　●　　●

One weekend, a month after her father'd left, her grandparents came to visit, and I stayed away. Not because I wanted to, but because Alice didn't meet me at the end of her driveway on either morning, so I headed home both times, and on the second morning, in the kitchen, my mother asked me: "How's Alice?"

"She's fine," I told her. "I don't really want to talk about it, actually." I poured myself some cereal.

"Well, then," she said.

I ate Captain Crunch, thinking about new strategies for

our rabbit hunts. My mom sipped coffee, flipped pages of the newspaper. No one could escape the war. Television and newspaper headlines: bombings, civilian deaths, terrorist organizations.

"I guess she doesn't really talk about it much," I said.

She set the newspaper down and took her glasses off. She was still in her pajamas. My mother seemed to me an ordinary person. She had none of the eccentricities of Alice or her parents. She worked at a bank, made a decent salary, and was always fair-minded and treated me like an adult. My father, really, was the same way. He, too, worked at a bank, though a different one, and often times, on weekends, he did his own thing.

"Listen, Ike," my mom said. "The important thing is that you're there for her. She's experiencing something unique to her. You'll never fully understand it. The best thing you can do is support her and be a good listener if she wants to talk, okay?"

My heart sank at the words "you'll never fully understand." Not because it was some new information, but because it was exactly what I'd been thinking about for the last month.

I got up and rinsed my bowl.

"Are you okay, Ike? Do you understand?"

"I'm fine," I said.

●　　●　　●

The summer days clipped by, like they always do, and in the nearly two months since her father'd been deployed, Alice and I had developed a feel for each other and the land. We worked slowly, methodically, silently around her property, sometimes twice. By now, we'd shot plenty of rabbits, including four tiny ones on one trip. There was a manic feeling about it, a feeling of unravelling helplessness, as if we were doing something we simultaneously hated, but also gave us some sense of accomplishment—collecting carcasses and burying them in the back part of her property; making progress toward her father's request. Neither of us loved it, I know that, but when we saw the young ones—the ones that had been causing the most damage to the gardens on account of their size and ability to get between the wire-mesh fence—there was a feeling of duty, necessity, and we acted accordingly. But the thing about the young ones, the tiny ones, unlike the adults, is that after we shot them, they flung their bodies all over the ground—flopping like a largemouth bass on the floor of a fishing boat—and sometimes the bunnies would flop for so long that Alice would take a stick and swat them over the head. After that, their eyes would bulge, and blood would be everywhere. At one point, we shot one and it skittered around for a few minutes before composing itself and crawling away into a thicket of grass, its back legs dragging behind while it motored forward with the front ones. We searched, but couldn't find it. The poor injured animal. I feel confident that we both felt a sense of dread. But that didn't last long. We saw another one soon after, and she brought the gun to her shoulder, in some automated response, and fired.

We were up to twenty-plus rabbits over the last six weeks, and still, rabbits were everywhere, most notably when Alice worked the gardens during the day, and would report back to me the various damage that was done: the tomato plants, the stem of an asparagus spear, the tops of the carrots and beets. I tried to help her with the garden work, but she refused my help. "You've already committed to one task," she told me, "and that's already too generous."

One afternoon, between our hunting excursions, I snuck up on her while she was in the garden. I stood out of sight, while she pulled weeds, her face protected by a sun hat. I was about to say something, ask if she needed help, but that's when I heard her sniffling and crying—weeping, really—and in that moment I wanted nothing more than to comfort her, to offer her some support. As I approached, she picked up a trowel and started stabbing the ground and crying even harder. Inconsolable sobs.

"Alice," I said.

"Go away, Ike," she said.

"Are you okay? Do you need help with this?"

"Go!" she said. I backed up a little, but stayed there hoping she'd say something else; hoping she'd change her mind and invite me in through the garden gate. "I'm fine!" She whipped her head in my direction. "Just go!"

● ● ●

That evening before bed my mother asked me again about Alice. "You two spend an awful lot of time together."

"Just hanging out in the yard," I said.

"Hanging out?"

"We're building something," I said. Which was partly true about the cemetery.

"Building something?" My mother sat on the living room couch. She'd been reading a book under weak lamp light.

"It's kinda like a fort," I said, "at the far side of their property."

"I see," my mom said.

"I saw her crying today," I said. "She yelled at me to leave."

"That doesn't mean she's mad at you, Ike. It just means she needs her own space."

"I kinda figured that."

"Has she mentioned anything about seeing Marcy?" Marcy was my mom's friend, a shrink.

"No, she hasn't said anything."

"Hmm, okay," she said. "Well, just don't bring it up to her, okay? Promise me, Ike?"

"Roger-that," I said.

"Excuse me?" my mother said.

"10-4, Private, Roger-that."

My mother laughed, waved me over for a hug. "You're such a silly boy," she said. "Goodnight, sweetheart."

●　　●　　●

The next morning, as we lay in the dewy grass waiting for a rabbit (we were trying a new strategy: baiting them with scraps of kitchen compost), I asked: "You know a woman named Marcy?"

"Maybe," she said. "Do you?"

"Probably," I said. "She's a shrink, the one I know. You see her?" I didn't want to make her feel bad by bringing it up. Rather, I wanted to show her in any way possible that I could be trusted.

"There," she said.

Alice brought the pellet gun up to her sights. "I don't see anything," I said.

"Wait 'til it moves toward us."

"There's nothing there."

"Wait it out," she said. "A closer shot equals better shot."

"Well you're close to me right now."

"So what's that supposed to mean—should I shoot you?"

"What's got into you?" I said.

"What's got into you? she said.

She stood up and the rabbit ran away. She walked to the barn, stashed her pellet gun in the corner. I got up, followed her, set the slingshot next to it.

"I've got a doctor appointment or something," she said. "Meet back later."

●　　●　　●

In mid-August the county fair came to town, and Alice and I took a few days off to enjoy the rides. We purchased wristbands that gave us unlimited access to everything. Alice liked the rides that made me puke, but I went on them anyway. On the second night of the fair, Alice and I were waiting in line when some older boys we knew distantly from school came up behind us. Three of them, all wearing polo shirts and goop in their hair that made it glisten. One said to Alice, "Hey, Alice."

Alice looked at him, crossed her arms over her chest, and turned back around.

"Remember me?" the kid said. "From the assembly? We sat next to each other."

The boys formed a hedge around her, and I was sort of shoved off to the side. I couldn't hear very well on account of the all the rides and people, but I heard them talk about their fathers. The boys smelled faintly of some kind of cologne. I stood there waiting for Alice in my Dr. Seuss t-shirt and hand-me-down denim shorts.

"We should talk sometime," one of the boys said to Alice.

"That'd be nice," she said. "It feels like there's no one else who understands, you know?"

"I do," he said.

They smiled at each other, and then the boys sauntered off around the corner. I stayed idle, waiting for Alice to make a move.

"Tilt-A-Whirl," she said, stepping in that direction.

"What was that about?" I said.

"Nothing much," she said.

●   ●   ●

The days following the carnival, Alice honed in on the rabbits. She renewed her resolve, and brought to our hunting excursions a cold, steady determination. She marched with a particular fervor; she took care when she aimed; she spent more time waiting in ambush. Gone were the days of flushing rabbits, stomping through grass, and taking shots at moving targets. "We killed all the dumb ones," she told me. "And now what's left is the cream of the crop, the top dogs, the fittest of the fit."

Meanwhile, her parents' garden looked healthy. The newly planted asparagus grew tall; the beans were a bit chewy, but plentiful; the green tomatoes were starting to grow pale, which meant they'd start ripening at any moment, and her mother, finally venturing out of the house, had started bringing their bounty to the Farmers Market.

Over the next few days, with her renewed determination, she slaughtered a dozen more rabbits. I no longer took shots. She was killing on her own now. A rabbit assassin. I simply collected the dead and buried them.

On one occasion, I'd already dug up the dirt and set a rabbit inside. I was beginning to cover it when she walked up with another. "I didn't hear you shoot," I said.

"Well I did."

"I'll put them in the same hole."

"Dig another," she said. "We need to keep track."

"This is getting ridiculous."

"You're ridiculous." She threw the rabbit at my feet. "If you don't want to help, I'll find someone else who doesn't backtalk orders."

"Like who?" I said. "Your boyfriend from the fair?"

"What are you talking about?"

"*Maybe we should talk sometime,*" I said in a mocking voice.

Her face bunched up. She pointed the pellet gun at me. "Say it again," she said. She brought the butt firm against her shoulder. She closed one eye and aimed for my chest. "Go on. Say it again tough guy."

"You don't have the balls to shoot me," I said. "Your old

man might, but not you."

"Fuck you, Ike," she said. "Say it again, and see what happens."

I could see her trembling now. I dropped the shovel and walked up to her so that my chest was only inches from the barrel. "Maybe we should talk sometime, that'd be so nice."

"God, I hate you." She threw the gun on the ground and stormed off.

"Alice," I said. "I'm sor—"

"I hate you!"

"Alice, wait."

●　　●　　●

"Heartfelt sincerity is what makes an apology an apology," my mother said to me.

We were at the grocery store, and I hadn't seen Alice for a few days. I felt awful, hollowed out and sick to my stomach. I held up the gifts I intended to give her.

"That's sweet, Ike," my mother said, "but don't bother with those. A girl like Alice doesn't want a card and a carnation. What she wants is for you to express how horrible you feel for making her feel the way you did, understand?"

I took the flower and card back to where I'd found them, and while doing that, I saw Alice's mother who stood in the produce aisle, inspecting a bag of grapes.

"Hello, Mr. Thurlow."

"Hi, Mrs. Thornburg."

"Are you and Alice not playing anymore?" She plucked a grape and popped it into her mouth.

"We haven't for a few days, did she mention something?"

"Kind of sour," she said. She set the grapes back, picked up another bunch, and tried another. The fluorescent lights made her look different. I knew she was younger than my mother, but the creases around her eyes seemed more pronounced. Her hair was unkempt. It occurred to me that I'd never seen her in this way, though I didn't think it looked bad. Just different. "Much better," she said to herself. She put the bag in the cart. "I haven't talked to Alice in a few days. We're having our differences. You too?"

"I think so," I said.

"Well don't wait too long to stop back. Whatever you two are doing in the backyard, she seems to miss. She hasn't been this grouchy in a while."

"I should get back," I said. "My mom's waiting for me."

"Ta-ta for now."

●　　●　　●

I went over to see her the next day, and before I could say anything, Alice came out of the house and said: "I've been stalking a couple young ones along the fence row in the southwest corner."

"I wanted to tell you something," I said.

"My dad warned me that once we start eliminating the ones living on our land, others might move in and try to take over on account of the fresh food source. I guess that makes sense, doesn't it?"

"Yeah that sounds right," I said. "But I wanted to say something—"

"Here," she said. "You left this." She handed me the sling shot, which I hadn't used in weeks, and the shovel, which I took and leaned against the barn. "Follow me," she said. "And when I give you the signal, crouch low to the ground. You take one end and I'll stalk them from over there."

She crouched low, tiptoeing to the opposite side. When she got into position, she looked back at me and smiled, put her thumb up to signal her approval. I waved, and without another word, we slipped back into our roles.

●　　●　　●

Late August turned into September—those summer days when the heat starts to wane, and the land, which had been so lush for so long, grows dull and yellow. By then the gardens were at peak: ripe tomatoes, melons, squash, cukes, beets, carrots, peas, beans, onions, and more, and Alice's mother was selling out at the market. Saturday morning in mid-September, after her mother had left for town, Alice and I picked a handful of carrots, rubbed the dirt and grit off on our shirts, and sat on top of the straw mulch and gnawed on them like rabbits at a buffet. After all, there were hardly any more left on the property. I'd lost count of how many we'd buried.

"We're predators," she said to me.

"Except we don't eat what we kill," I said. "Which makes us—"

"Killers," she said. I could tell it was something she'd been thinking about.

"Maybe," I said. "I was going to say it makes us... *inhumane*."

"I'm getting tired of this," she said.

"Roger-that," I said.

It was the first either of us had mentioned it, yet we continued on as if there were no other choice. It was a time in our lives when our commitment to authority—in this case her father—outweighed how we ourselves felt about the task at hand.

"Maybe we should be eating the rabbits," I said.

"But I don't know how to clean them or anything."

"I do," I said. "Learned from my grandpa. I could dress one if you'd like—if you don't think it'd be too disgusting."

●　　●　　●

The next rabbit we killed, we gutted and skinned under the shade of a willow tree using one of her dad's bowie knives, and together we took turns ripping out the guts, dissecting and figuring out what was what: lungs, liver, heart. Of course the intestines were easy to locate, and the entire thing smelled horrific. After we were done determining internal body parts, I sliced out sections of meat, and arranged it on a piece of plywood.

Alice found a cast iron kettle with a stand, and we mounted it over a fire that she had made in the backyard, not far from the gardens. She dumped some oil in the kettle, wiped out the rusty residue with a rag, and then dumped more oil into it, and after it was sufficiently heated, she cut off some sprigs of sage and rosemary from their herb garden and let that simmer for a minute before she dumped the meat inside.

"You know what you're doing," I said.

"I've seen my mom and dad cook enough."

"When's he coming back?"

"I'm not exactly sure."

"You can talk to me anytime," I said. "You know that, right?"

She nodded, poked at the fire with a stick.

"The rabbit shouldn't take long to cook," I said.

"Apparently he's over there making sure innocent people don't get hurt by landmines or faulty equipment. He's making sure people are safe. He's not one of those guys over there with a gun killing people."

We both sat there and watched the rabbit cook. The smell was both delicious and off-putting, the aroma of herbs mixed with a slight twinge of its innards. While we waited for it to finish, a mid-size bunny came into sight along the edge of the prairie grass. I noticed it, but didn't say anything. I think Alice noticed as well, but she didn't mention it either, and I think we both realized then that we didn't want to kill anymore. Or at least that's what I imagined. It was then that I started asking her questions, trying to make up some conversation about cooking, until finally, the bunny—the one alive at the edge of the property—found cover and refuge, prolonging its life for at least one more night.

But the next day we killed and buried that young one. We thought it might've been the last one on their property because after that we hunted two more days without seeing anything else. It was then that Alice decided to widen our hunting territory into the neighborhoods that butted up against the edge of town, just north of their property.

"Town bunnies are stupid and easy prey," she said.

"I think we should be done," I said. "Trespassing doesn't sound fun."

"My father would be doubly impressed if we doubled the size of our cemetery."

●　　●　　●

In the early evening hours, when families were inside getting ready for bed, Alice and I stalked the backyards of a neighborhood within walking distance of her house, and we—she—started shooting rabbits near gardens and bushes. I didn't bother with the slingshot, but instead, brought along a burlap sack, and together we developed a new system: running and ducking behind garages and sheds, and individual bushes and hedges that made up and divided backyards. She'd shoot and kill, and I'd scoop them into the sack. Within a few weeks—by early October—we'd almost doubled the cemetery count, which was starting to look like an actual cemetery given all the mini-rock piles that marked each site.

Early mornings were our most productive time, but we also hunted the occasional evening if we finished our homework promptly after school. One Wednesday night, with a lot of houses empty on account of church, we ventured into a new area. The evening came upon us quickly, which sometimes happens in the fall. We had yet to see a rabbit, so Alice wanted to try for a few more minutes. We crouched along a row of arborvitaes, out of the house's line of sight. We got to the end of the row before we saw it sitting there in the middle of someone's yard, huddled up against the cold dusk. She took aim and I readied the bag. The pellet gun cracked the air, and as soon as that happened, we heard a loud shriek. I peered around her, and a cat was flopping on the ground. We ran up to it. Alice re-pumped the pellet gun. The cat hissed. Blood dripped from its nose and mouth. It had a collar around its neck, and just as Alice was about to put it out of its misery, someone shouted, "Get outta here!"

We startled, ran back behind the arborvitaes, past a tool shed, through a row of backyards, between two houses, around the corner, and up the hill to her house. We stopped at the end of her driveway.

"Holy shit," Alice said. "Did you see that?"

"See what?" I said.

"The collar. It was someone's pet."

Fall pushed into late fall, and I helped her and her mother harvest the last acorn and butternut squash before cutting out the vines and putting them into a burn pile. We prepped the gardens for colder weather, which meant general clean up, covering the bare soil with leaves, and after that Alice and I didn't see each other much except for at school.

Alice and I never talked about that summer and fall hunting the rabbits. Even now, there are times I've thought of bringing it up to her, but simply haven't found the courage to do so. Just a week ago, at our high school graduation, sitting beside her—as our last names had destined us to do since the day she moved to town—Alice and I talked and laughed, but that was all.

Once, in the fall of our senior year, attending the same party where she'd had too much to drink, she pulled me out of the crowd, out of the loud music, and melted into me, crying into my shoulder. I didn't know if she was happy or sad or something else entirely. But she held me, and I felt the shape of her body against me, and even today, several months later, I can still recall what that felt like. I thought of asking her what was the matter, but that question, I think, would've cheapened our moment, lessened it somehow. And I was content simply holding her.

After two deployments over the course of five years, Alice's father would eventually return permanently, but things were different. He rarely ventured outside, and his military body became soft and slow. He drank more.

The few times I saw him out and about, he tried to sound upbeat, tried to carry a conversation, asking me about school and sports, but I could tell right away that he'd lost that bounce in his step, that fervor that made him who he was. He wasn't the same man who'd given Alice and me enthusiastic orders to protect the gardens.

And just a few nights ago, at Alice's graduation party, I excused myself from the crowd of people, and stood alone in the backfield where we had buried all those rabbits, and watched as the first of the fireflies floated out of the grass—their neon flashes a distinct reminder of our time there only six years ago. The rock piles that marked each gravesite are long gone.

We had cleared those away the following spring after we had finished the sixth grade, and after Alice realized her father's deployment would be extended. She had understood finally that he wouldn't be there to see what we'd accomplished for him. She told me she was tired of seeing those piles of brown and gray stones, so one evening we cleared the gravesites. We moved the rocks to the edge of her property, where eventually they would disappear under the tall grasses that would grow over and around them. It was tempting to count the total number of dead rabbits, to see what we'd accomplished, but after I'd observed Alice, with her slumped shoulders and heavy feet, I opted not to bring it up.

As we finished our chore, one that we'd started and finished without talking, Alice sat on the ground next me, and said, "All those rabbits, and only one casualty of war."

It was then that I thought of the cat—its high-pitched squawk and desperate hiss—the way it flung the last efforts of its body up in the air and on the ground, fighting for one last chance, all the muscle confusion and disorientation. It had wanted to run away, no doubt, but when its mind tried to communicate that to its body, there was only one reaction it could muster until finally it had nothing left.

Alice got up from where we were sitting. She held one last rock, and while she talked about throwing it into the field, she didn't. She sat back down and rested her arms in her lap. The sky darkened and bats fluttered above. The grass grew cool and damp. And though we were young, just finished with the sixth grade, I think we were both perfectly aware, sitting there among the mess of buried rabbit carcasses, that there had been far more casualties in the past year than either of us wanted to admit.

A
BASKETBALL
STORY

Twins, Jake and Danny, spend their summer days on a concrete basketball slab behind their house shooting hoops, playing horse, playing pig, playing around-the-world, playing one-on-one. It has been a warm summer already, and, according to their father, it will only get worse, so they get up early, before the sunshine makes its way to that part of the yard, to practice, and then again in the evenings, when the sun has faded behind the large sugar maple that towers over everything. It is the summer after the sixth grade, and the boys have goals, all of which involve basketball; all of which involve sweat and hard work; all of which they have solemnly vowed to the other that they would attain together.

The one goal first and foremost in their minds is to be exactly like their older brother, Gabe, who is taller than they are, who will always be taller, and is, according to their father, a pure shooter. Whatever pure means, they aren't sure, but they are working every day, nonetheless, to improve their skills. No one else, including their father, mother, or Gabe, knows of their goals. Everything between the boys, without question, is a secret, unless otherwise conferred with the other. It has always been like this: a tight lipped intimacy that the parents mumble about, and Gabe questions, but no one, including the twins, fully understands.

Gabe is a 6'1" shooting guard who started his junior year on one of the best high school basketball teams in Iowa. (Okay, so it's Iowa, better known for wrestling, hog farms, and polluted drinking water, but they are not from rural Iowa, they are from Cedar Rapids, a town pushing two hundred thousand, with urban renewal that rivals Detroit, thanks to a major flood, and maybe more gym space per capita than anywhere else in the state). Gabe is getting scholarship looks from mid-majors, and their father is pushing him to one of these universities since he will probably "see playing time right away." Which might not happen if he were to attend a Big-Ten school like the University of Iowa, a school that other teams, "mop the floor with," according to their father. These conversations usually occur when the family is seated at the dinner table picking at a variety of their mother's dishes: fried rice, fish, chicken adobo, and leftover lasagna. Their father, with one helping from each entree, will wink and pat Gabe on the back as they discuss basketball moments: his own and Gabe's, certainly, but sometimes Gabe will mention a professional player, say, Jordan or Magic or Bird. Their father prefers the big men of basketball so he is usually talking about Kareem's sky hook or Robert Parish's presence, or Keven McKale's goofy face.

The three boys, the twins and Gabe, come from a Caucasian father and a Filipino mother. Their parents met when their father, a former Naval Officer, was stationed in the Philippines circa late 60s. The twins are not tall, like their mother, but they are strong and athletic. They hardly speak to anyone, including each other. This is another trait from their mother who, by choice, also hardly speaks to anyone unless she is on the phone with her friends, who all talk in Tagalog. The twins enjoy silence. They are comfortable—actually, prefer—being together with very few actual words, because they have developed a system through which they can communicate complicated information using sideways glances, or the squinting of eyes, or other non-verbal forms. This used to frustrate their father, a tall confident man with sun-toned skin, a bullhorn voice, and a large charismatic, back-slapping personality, but his wife, their mother, assures him and Gabe that everything is fine and that the boys are perfectly normal, and the one point that helps assure their father is that the boys seem to love basketball—which they do—and want to be like Gabe. Which they do.

Like their father, Gabe tries to coach the boys when they do not want to be coached. They want to be like him, yes, but they do not want to hear him yell about their improper form or technique, and they do not want him to teach them, when all they want to do is shoot around and play with one another. Gabe tells them that he is offering them lessons, for free, will teach them the art of basketball, for free, and how to get open shots, if only they would listen. This happens once a week, maybe twice, before Gabe gets frustrated and goes into the house or shoots on his own, ignoring the boys. Sometimes, he and their father will shoot together, and while looking at them from the back, with the exception of their father's broader-set shoulders, they are almost indistinguishable. They are the same height, have the same voice, and command the same attention when stepping into a room, or onto the court. The twins, however: their collective presence in any place, at any time, occupies hardly any space, affecting hardly any people. They are small in stature, short, diminutive, soft-spoken. Each is their mother's son. She, herself: short, gentle. And the twins know that in the future they might still be meek and quiet, small and diminutive. In looks, in stature, in everything. They are not angry about it. Not yet anyway, and they might not ever be. If they were alone, without the other, perhaps so. Perhaps one, alone, might suffer from something such as envy. But they have each other, and this, it seems to them now, will always be enough.

● ● ●

The slab on which they play ball was poured by their father and some of his friends on a cool spring night in May, over ten years ago, initially for himself and Gabe. The basketball hoop is square, fiberglass, with a breakaway rim for those who can dunk, like Gabe and his friends, and the slab extends as far as the three point line at the top but does not extend as far on the sides. Gabe, consequently, is not as adept at shooting baseline three-pointers, which is something that greatly frustrates their father as he will occasionally pull up the excel sheet that tracks where on the court during the varsity games Gabe has taken shots, broken down by baseline right, baseline left, in the paint, top of the key, and behind the arc, top, elbow, and baseline, and it is on the baseline threes that show a dramatic increase in missed shots. Over ten percentage points.

It is for this reason that Gabe stands at the edge of the baseline, where the concrete lip meets a bed of landscaping rocks, pretty rocks, which filter onto the grass. Gabe stands on these rocks while the twins rebound for him. Once he shoots, one of the boys passes him a ball while the other rebounds, so that there are always two balls going at once. Gabe stands in place, catching the ball, his fingers instinctively finding the grooves, as he fires up shot after shot, a pure, perfect form, as each ball goes swoosh through the net and bounces onto the concrete. He is mostly set-shooting which means he is not elevating in the air—a jump shot—but this is fine, according to their father, because it is important to develop a rhythm and get used to eyeing a shot from that distance.

Gabe continues to shoot, the boys continue to rebound, and the sun starts to creep over the house and onto the concrete slab, and after what feels to the twins like an hour, they announce that it's time for a break. Gabe instructs them to stay, tells them that he's just getting started, but the twins have, without talking, agreed to go inside, so instead of rebounding and firing the balls back, they let them roll into the grass, behind the hoop, and they start for the door. Locusts screech. The day is humid. The boys have not done any of their own shooting or passing or playing, but their t-shirts are soaked. "This is what Dad's talking about," Gabe tells the boys. "And the reason you guys can't get over the hump." They have heard this before, from their father, this notion of getting over the hump, going from good to great, or, like Gabe, becoming a *pure shooter*. The twins walk into the house while Gabe mumbles insults: "Worthless pieces of shit, suck at basketball, will never get any better with that lazy-ass work ethic."

●　　●　　●

The days continue: June into July, and pretty soon, August, a month in which Gabe's team has signed up for tournaments throughout the Midwest. It is a limited roster, up to eight boys per team, but their father has made the decision to bring only the top seven kids on their high school squad, and because this is not a school sanctioned event, their father acts as head coach, which he does with a slightly elevated fervor from his years of backyard coaching. In preparation for the tournament, which is two hours west in Des Moines, Gabe is shooting constantly, every day, three times a day, and the twins are ordered, by Gabe and their father, to be active rebounders, to pass the ball well so that Gabe can catch and shoot in rhythm, and this, their father tells them, is good practice, because of their height deferential, they'll probably be stuck playing point guard which is a position that Gabe can play, if needed, but why would anyone waste a pure shooter's wrist on dribbling?

One after another, after another, Gabe works his way from the pebbled baseline to the top of the key and back down the opposite baseline and back again. The twins' passes, even Gabe acknowledges, are good—they pack a punch, they rotate well, but not too much, they travel straight, and because of this, Gabe praises them. When they are finished, they play two-on-one which is something they have done all summer, and the twins, devising ways to score on Gabe, have developed a system—a Stockton to Malone, a Pippen to Jordan, a Magic to Kareem-like chemistry. The goal has never been to beat Gabe, but to simply score one basket because, as Gabe promises, if they do, he will buy them each a malt at the Dairy Queen. But Gabe is too good, too quick, and knows every play in the book, backward and forward. The boys try to shoot, but Gabe blocks them. The boys try to double team him, but he dribbles between his legs, around them, crosses-over, re-crosses-over (because he can) and jumps into the air, and once he reaches peak elevation, he flicks his wrist, the ball moves off his fingertips in a perfect arc, rotation, motion. The follow through is impeccable, a hand-in-the-cookie-jar, their father used to say, and the ball barely touches the net. The games the twins play against Gabe are always to five points, and every game, since they have started, have been five-nil, and after Gabe shoots and sinks his fourth point, he likes to tease them a little, dribble around, through their legs, and back again, and on this particular occasion he gets all the way to the hoop, but misses on purpose, a brick off the side of the rim, just to extend the game. One of the twins takes it back to the top of the key, the other picks for him—a pick and roll—and Gabe, the boys observe, seems to know what is happening before they do. He shuffles his feet, sees that the boy dribbling is actually going to try to pass around him, to his brother who is "rolling" to the basket. "Come on," Gabe says to the boys, "you gotta do better than that." He puts his foot out to stop the pass, but he overextends, he reaches too far. He has overestimated what the boys can actually do, so as he reaches with his right foot, his legs open, his groin pulls slightly, and the ball goes between his legs and into the hands of the other boy, who is standing five feet from the rim, he catches the pass, Gabe pulls up lame, and the boy sinks the shot.

● ● ●

The twins are equally terrified of what may come of this, but when their father gets home and sees Gabe on the couch icing his groin, he says, "How bad?" Gabe says it's not too bad, that he can walk. He thinks it's a slight strain, a minor pull, and their father says, rest on it for a week, and we'll see how you feel come tournament time. The twins are relieved. Mom is relieved. Their father, if he is not relieved, is hiding it.

For dinner, their mother makes some version of the usual: rice, chicken adobo, steamed vegetables. A cordless phone is tucked between her ear and shoulder, as she speaks to a friend in Tagalog, a language that is familiar to the twins and Gabe, not because of their mother, but because it is a close cousin to Spanish, and they pick up phrases: "Como esta," is the one that stands out most.

Dinner is a quiet affair. The kitchen smells of the salty adobo mix and cabbage. Mom and Dad and Gabe create some semblance of conversation. The twins fork silently into their food. They like it, and sometimes, similar to their mother, they eat with their hands, but not often because their father does not approve. Meanwhile, their mother enjoys it, and encourages them. Toward the end of the meal, while the twins are still gnawing on their chicken bones, their father looks at them for a moment, wipes his mouth with a napkin, and asks, finally: "What the hell happened today?" The twins stop eating. They make eye contact. They tell each other that their father wants to find someone to blame for Gabe's strain. Their father's tone suggests that he has been thinking about this since he has been home. The twins look down at their food, their mother continues eating. The only person who can address this in a satisfactory way is Gabe. And just as the twins are about to get up and leave the table, Gabe speaks up.

"Just shooting around in back with the boys," Gabe says.

Their father shakes his head. He appears to want to say more. He has told Gabe in the past not to "jack-around" with the twins for fear of something exactly like this, but he and Gabe rarely bicker, or argue, or find any point to disagree on, so their father just continues to shake his head while Gabe clears his plate. Their mother pinches food and sets it into her mouth. Between bites, she asks the boys a few questions. She asks: *how was your day?* She asks: *did you get some good shots in?* She asks: *did you do your chores?* But they are too focused on finishing their own chicken, eating the rest as fast as possible, before going off to their room to sit with each other in private. If they feel up to it, they might talk about the day's events, Dad, Gabe, and how much they love their mother's food.

● ● ●

Gabe is sidelined, restricted to play, restricted to shoot, restricted to do anything, as a rule stated by their father. The twins carry on without their older brother. They pass and shoot, play one-on-one, and dribble around the court, and while it is clear that they want to be as good as Gabe, it is equally known that neither wants to be better than the other, so they practice and push each other, shot after shot, follow through after follow through, soaking their t-shirts with sweat before 10 a.m. But in their games of one-on-one, horse, and around-the-world, they take turns winning. Each knows the other's game better than their own—the way the other dribbles; the way they go to the hoop; the way they dip the ball below their chin, as if to gain momentum, before shooting. They know all of this in the same way they know what the other looks like while dead asleep, something each boy would never know about himself. They play in silence, focused on their passes, their shots, their all-around game, and while neither of them acknowledges this, they both enjoy having the court to themselves. As the hours and days tick by, as they move around the horn passing and shooting, playing one-on-one, it seems that the twins finally understand what their father and Gabe mean when they talk about a shooting zone, or feeling the ball, or finding a rhythm. For the twins, there is relief knowing that, as they improve significantly, they are more certain about their own and collective prowess on the court—that individually they are significant, but together they will be unstoppable.

●　●　●

On the day before the tournament, the twins are outside dribbling around the concrete slab, taking shots. The bouncing balls echo off the house, making a sound that the boys have come to appreciate, if not love. They shoot on their own, in silence, always in silence, as the sun beats down on their already tan shoulders and necks. Gabe is not home, he is at the grocery store, at their parents' request, purchasing Gatorade and Power Bars for the weekend. His groin seems okay, not great, but okay, and he says he's ready to go this weekend. The boys are out back when they hear a vehicle pull into their driveway. The sound of which is nothing like any of the three vehicles driven by their parents or Gabe. A low steady bass comes from the speakers. The twins look at each other warily, and each, without talking, turns toward the driveway to check on this disturbance, a Nissan Pathfinder. Out saunters Joe Jackson Jr, the other D-I prospect on the Washington Warrior basketball team, 6'3", slender, light black skin and immaculately formed hair. The boys want to think "combed" hair, but they are not sure at this point how a black man combs his hair. At school, they have seen kids, friends, pick at their hair, and subsequently leave the picks in their hair, but never with any actual combing, but now, they notice that the waves in Joe Jackson Jr's hair seem too perfectly placed to be any sort of accident.

"What's good, boys?" Joe Jackson Jr says. "Where's GD?" The twins have to register Gabriel David before remembering that David is Gabe's middle name. Joe puts his hands in the air, signaling for one of them to pass the ball. There is a brief moment of reorientation that takes place on the court. It is probably unnoticeable to Joe, but it is there, and it hangs in the air, this decision, until Joe Jackson Jr claps his hands together, interrupting the line of silent communication between the boys. Before it is conferred by both, Jake fires a pass to Joe Jackson Jr, and Danny looks at him, questioning why it was Jake and not himself, and it occurs to Danny, in that moment, that Jake's jump shot might be a bit stronger than his own, something he has not said aloud, or even acknowledged to himself, or Jake, until this very moment, and that idea, that Jake might be making progress toward something that Gabe and their father call a sweet stroke, something they suggest can be used on the basketball court and with the honeys, causes Danny to turn away, grab another ball, and shoot on his own.

Joe dribbles around them and pulls up at the free throw line. The boys watch the ball leave his fingertips, the slow back spin, the perfect arc, the inevitable outcome, which sounds exactly as they refer to it: swoosh. Jake rushes over and passes the ball back to Joe who puts up another, then another, and another, until finally he asks when Gabe will be back.

"Soon," Jake says. "He's at the store."

Danny looks at him in shock and awe as Jake has shown more interest in talking to Joe Jackson Jr than he has to anyone else that he can remember.

"Let's see some shots," Joe says. Joe seems genuinely interested in the twins, and Jake puts up a few that clank off the rim, while Danny stands at the side of the concrete slab with the ball in his palm. "Ain't you gonna shoot, youngster?"

Joe says to Danny, but Danny cannot find the words to express himself. He wants to address his thoughts and words toward Jake, who has now made an immediate leap past him into some new social and athletic realm, but instead of saying anything, Danny drops the ball and walks toward the house. Joe picks up the ball, and just before Danny goes inside, he hears Joe say to Jake, "What's up with that fool?"

"Who knows?" Jake says.

● ● ●

Joe Jackson Jr stays the night at their house. He eats Filipino food and comments on how good it is. He engages everyone in conversation, he looks them in the eye when he speaks, he is effortlessly who he is, and who he is, Danny believes, is everything Jake wants to be. Jake wants to shoot hoops with him; show him their room; watch television with him; ask him questions about basketball, school, girls. It is confusing and indescribable to Danny, who sits on the sidelines and watches as this happens so quickly, so suddenly, that he is now altogether unsure of his position within the family, when his position has always been unquestioned: he is, simply, one of the twins. Now, he is still one of the twins, but he feels, in just a few hours, that he has been cut off from some source, some vital energy, something he needs. He has been cut off from his twin, his brother, but for Danny it is more than that, because Danny feels as though he has been cut off from an essential part of himself. He watches as Joe and Gabe shoot around on the concrete slab, the sun finding space behind the old maple. He sees how Jake has cottoned to, and is hanging on, every word, every action, every inaction, of Joe Jackson Jr, and now all Danny can think about is getting past this weekend to a time when they can resume life as it was, and is, supposed to be.

● ● ●

The next day they leave for the weekend, and this is the part the twins are used to: getting dragged to various tournaments around the Midwest, watching Gabe, trying to "learn the game," as their father has suggested, but mostly they like to eat popcorn and hotdogs. Except now, at this tournament, in Des Moines, Jake is interested in watching Gabe and Joe play. He is interested in their moves, their shots, how they move when they do not have the ball. It's artistic, Jake says. Danny is sure that his brother has heard that term from someone else, trying it out for his own use, and Danny would admit, too, although not to anyone else, including Jake, that they—Gabe and Joe—are something to watch: the way they catch and shoot in one slick motion, the cross-over dribble, the help-defense. It is easy enough for Danny to admit that Gabe and Joe are spectacular to watch, the best back court combination in the tournament, and it is no surprise to anyone that at the end of the day on Sunday, their team will be crowned champions, and everything will go according to plan, everyone will be in a wonderful mood, and they will drive home in the dark. And that does happen, but with one exception. Gabe, in the last game, reinjures his groin, and is forced to sit out the last quarter of the game, but it does not matter because the team is "just that good." Gabe sulks on the way home, happy to be crowned champion, and earning co-MVP of the tournament with Joe Jackson Jr, but his joy is mitigated by every slight movement which keeps him grimacing on the ride home. Joe offers him upbeat condolences, and assures him that he'll be fine by season, which is true, but for now, no one in the car is thinking about season, and their victory has been somewhat overshadowed. Their father does not speak on the ride home, except to congratulate them, and their mother does not speak either. Danny tries to sleep, and Jake replays every series of every game with Joe Jackson Jr, until finally, much to everyone's relief, Gabe says, "Will you shut the hell up already."

For the next couple of weeks, before the start of school, Joe Jackson Jr quickly becomes a mainstay at their household, and Mom, Dad, Gabe, and Jake, it seems to Danny, could not be more thrilled. He shares meals, watches TV, lounges in the living room, and sometimes stays the night. He uses the guest bedroom which now has the lived in feel of Gabe's room, and has the unique smell of Joe Jackson Jr which the twins cannot quite name, but they simply think of as Joe.

Jake and Danny continue their quiet quest of becoming like their older brother, but it is different now, strained, and, in some instances, forced. Also, on occasion, Danny will find Jake hanging out with Gabe and Joe. It is not clear to either boy why Joe is hanging out at their house with such frequency, but it does not matter, it only matters that Jake finds it thrilling while Danny finds it intrusive.

One night in bed, a night that Joe is staying over in the guest room, Jake says to Danny, "What's going on?" On the surface it appears a simple question, but its actual meaning is not lost on Danny.

"We have a complete stranger living with us."

"He's cool," Jake says. "He's one of Gabe's best friends."

Danny turns to face the wall. He hears Jake get out of bed, and he wonders for a moment if Jake is going to crawl in with him, which is something they used to do—sometimes still do—when one is bothered and cannot sleep, which is how Danny is feeling now. But instead, Jake flips on the lamp on his desk and sits up in bed. "Danny," Jake says. He turns over so that he is facing Jake. Their room is a square with twin beds on opposite walls and two desks in between and two dressers on the opposite side, near the door. "Gabe said we need to start branching out a bit. He said we need to stop being so attached and stuff, always doing things together and with no one else."

Danny turns back onto his side so that he is facing the wall once more. He feels the warm wet drops form in his eyes, and he blinks them out so that they run down the bridge of his nose and temple, and onto the sheet. He peels off the blanket. After all, it is summer, and it is hot, and air conditioning on the top floor of an old two-story home does not work well. Jake clicks the light off, and Danny can hear him tucking himself under his own sheet.

Late in the night, after waiting for everyone to fall into their deep soundless sleeps, Danny tip-toes out of their room, down the stairs, and into the kitchen. It is cooler on the main floor where his mom and dad sleep. He is angry at Gabe for what he told Jake, but he is mostly mad at Joe Jackson Jr. Danny flips on the light. His feet feel cold and clammy on the oak floor, and his muscles are tired and weak. His hands shake, but not from being cold. He opens a drawer and looks down at the shiny metal. He handles a butcher's knife, its weight significant in his hand. He thinks it could be easy. Its sharp edges never betraying him. He sets the knife on the counter, turns around to get a glass of water. His throat is dry, and when he sets his cup down, his mother is standing in the doorframe, eyes half-closed and hair messy with sleep.

She says, "I thought I heard something in here. Go to sleep now, sweetie." She turns off the light, walks to her son, pulls him close. She is only an inch taller than the boys, the twins, but her presence feels marked, and in the still night air, with only the stars to light the rooftops, Danny's legs give way, and he whimpers quietly while his mother holds him.

●　　●　　●

Late August, the dog days, fuzzy-humid skies, the green puffs of leafed-out branches shimmering in a light breeze. Danny looks out the window. Gabe is in a lawn chair icing his injury, and Joe Jackson Jr is touching Jake's shooting arm, tucking his elbow in closer to his body. Jake's form has all of a sudden changed, has become more sophisticated. Joe Jackson Jr stands under the hoop while Jake takes consecutive shots: five from the baseline, five from the elbow, five from the free throw line. It looks a little bit like "around-the-world" except they are not alternating, that is, not until Jake has gone around the horn and back again, at which point, he switches spots with Joe, so that Jake is now the rebounder, and Joe fires up swoosh after swoosh, while Jake smiles, mouthing the words, "nice one," and firing the ball back at Joe with perfect passing form—a hard step forward, two hands on the ball, and a flick of both wrists so that the thumbs point down when the ball leaves Jake's hands. Joe catches the ball, shoots, and swoosh, five in a row, just like that, and then he side-shuffles to the free throw line. Their bodies glisten with sweat.

Danny puts on his high tops and readies himself to go out the door, but as he is tying up his laces, Joe and Jake come into the house, dripping sweat, smelling of the sun and the outdoors. Joe says to Danny, "What's up, cuz?" and Jake just gives him a cool head nod. While Joe and Jake are at the sink guzzling water, Danny tightens his laces and walks out into the blistering heat. He picks up the ball, but it feels different, foreign, and he knows that the other two might be inside watching. Gabe is still in the lawn chair.

"You doing all right, youngster?" Gabe says to Danny. Danny gives a slight, insignificant shrug, probably too subtle for Gabe to notice. Danny dribbles the ball, fires up a few shots. He becomes self-conscious of his form. He tries to tuck his elbow in; he tries to make the proper adjustments; he misses his first twenty attempts. Gabe encourages him, but Danny drops the ball and leaves the court.

● ● ●

That night, Danny is in the bathroom when he hears his mother ask Gabe, "Is everything okay with the boys?" By which she means Jake and Danny. Gabe says, "I think so, why?" She explains her concerns, and Danny finds some relief in her recognizing the growing distance between him and Jake. He thinks that perhaps she might help, that she might talk with Jake, or, better yet, Gabe might talk with Jake and suggest spending more time with his brother, but Gabe does not say that, he says something else entirely. He says, "I wouldn't worry about it. It's good for them to spend time apart. It's good for them to interact with others. They can't be together forever." But *together forever* is exactly what Danny thinks. It is not so much that he imagines his *entire* life with Jake, it is that he has not yet imagined his life *without* his brother, and this, for Danny, is the most worrisome of all: that Jake might find others to talk with, hang out with, and become friends with. Danny, in a moment of quiet anger, decides he does not need any of them. He decides he can do all of this on his own. He decides, quite adamantly, that he will meet other people and show everyone his new self.

● ● ●

Danny rides the city bus to the mall, alone. It is a Saturday afternoon, four days before school starts, and everyone will be there shopping. His plans are to see people, talk with people, use his allowance to buy something for himself, and after that, he will purchase lunch at the food court. A decision, he understands, that Jake usually makes for them. He has not told anyone of his whereabouts, only that he was going to go "out." To which Jake and Gabe did not respond, because they probably thought, by "out" he meant, "out back," to shoot hoops.

It is 3 p.m., and Danny walks around the mall, looking at hats, shoes, saying "hi" to familiar, sun-kissed faces. He buys an Orange Julius and skirts the edges of the walkways until he is slurping the bottom. He tries on jeans, shorts, t-shirts, dress shirts, and he talks with salesclerks and other people old enough to be his mom or dad or one of his grandparents. It is an odd feeling—talking with others—but on some level, without anyone else to witness these conversations, he feels emboldened. Ready for his new life. The air-conditioned space feels good at first, but almost as soon as he's getting comfortable, he starts to feel itchy and restless; stale and claustrophobic. He wants to leave immediately, but he has only been gone for a couple of hours, and he has not yet eaten at the food court, and he has not yet visited all of the stores he would like to visit. He sits on a bench and watches families and older teens who probably know Gabe. He rests his legs and plots his next move, which is to go to a video game arcade, and spend his remaining money. He will eat at another time.

● ● ●

He walks across the parking lot wearing his new Bulls cap. As the heat rises off the blacktop, sweat starts to form on his brow, and it occurs to him that this is the longest he has ever been away from his brother, Jake, who, by now, Danny imagines, is wondering and worrying where he is. He imagines his conversation with Gabe: "We need to go find him. Where is he? Why aren't you worried?" To which Gabe might reply: "Relax, this is good for you." But another scenario is just as plausible: Gabe, Jake, and Joe Jackson Jr shooting hoops, dribbling, passing—getting better at basketball. A trio of like-minded, pure-shooting, sweet-stroking hoopsters. Danny walks into the arcade. It is dark, damp, and cool. He changes in one of his five dollar bills, money he had been saving for dinner, and listens to all the quarters clang into the half-oval shaped space with the flapping metal lid. He looks around, trying to figure out where to start.

An hour, two hours, three hours slip by without his noticing. He is not always playing a game, but sometimes watching or talking with other, more experienced, gamers. He is out of money, save for his bus fare home. He is watching a person shoot Alien-like figures with a plastic Uzi when he feels alarmingly unsettled, off-kilter, almost light-headed. He is tired. Tired of people, tired of talking. If he were in the presence of Jake, he might curl up on the thin dank carpet and sleep. A long, much needed sleep. But right now, he is simply tired of himself, of being by himself, and being away from his brother. He mopes away from the flashing screens. He walks out the door into the early evening heat.

● ● ●

As he trots up the driveway, sporting his new Bulls cap, Danny hears bouncing basketballs and voices from behind the house. Joe Jackson Jr's SUV is parked out front. But that is okay. He does not care about Joe Jackson Jr or Gabe or his parents. Danny hurries around to the backyard and sees Gabe and Joe shooting, while Jake is underneath the hoop rebounding. The twins see each other. They meet somewhere near the edge of the court, on the pebbled rock border. They stand next to each other.

"Where you been, youngster?" Gabe says.

Danny tells him, with few words as possible, about the mall and the arcade.

Gabe says, "Good for you."

Joe Jackson Jr says, "Nice hat, cuz."

The twins stand together, watching the other two gather their balls and walk inside for a water break.

● ● ●

Now, the boys are alone, together, and collectively, they feel something like relief, but it is more than that. Something only they can know and feel. They stand near each other and absorb each other's presence. There are no pretenses; no need for words or touching; no need for explanations. It is understood. They stand, shoulder-to-shoulder, until one of them leans forward, taking the first step toward the court, and the other falls in stride, as if they have it timed out, as if they were instantly resynced, recalibrated, rejoined.

Jake dribbles to the back corner of the court, passes the ball to Danny—a give and go—and Danny sends him a bounce pass as Jake angles toward the hoop. The pass is pristine. Jake takes the ball, scoops it into his hands, and rises up for a layup. He rebounds his own shot, passes back to Danny, who shoots and misses, but this is okay, because Jake rebounds the ball, and passes back to Danny, who stands near the edge of the court, waiting for the pass, poised and ready for another shot.

IMAGINARY ENEMIES

Elbow and I ducked out of our nephew's birthday party and drove to Walmart to check on ammo prices. I didn't care about ammo prices. I was along for the ride. Elbow was married to my sister and just out of the Marine Corps. His hair was still high and tight, and he strutted around with a purposeful intensity that I had a difficult time keeping up with.

He stood at the ammo display, which was closed and fortified with a brass lock. He peered at the inventory. "Figures," he said. "They're out of .22 and 9 mil—everywhere in America's out of .22 and 9 mil." He put his hands on his hips and looked around. I stood behind him, pretending to care. .22, 9 mil? I had no idea. All I'd ever shot was a Red Rider BB gun at a friend's twelfth birthday party. Elbow glanced at the clerk. "Shit's going gangbusters with the current anti-gun, anti-ammo administration." The clerk—a dopey-eyed teenager with spots of acne—nodded and then went back to reading his *Fur-Fish-Game* magazine. Elbow marched over to the counter. The clerk looked up.

"When's the next shipment?" Elbow said.

"Tuesday," the clerk said. He spoke slow as an elephant. "But all the dudes in this department buy up the ammo and sell it for a premium."

"Fucking horseshit," Elbow said. He fidgeted with his hands, then leaned over the glass counter and plucked the magazine from the clerk.

"Dude," the clerk said. "I work in Auto. They just sent me over here to cover the desk while everyone's on break. I know nothing."

Elbow handed back the magazine.

"Hey," he said to the clerk. "Look alive." Elbow jabbed toward the clerk's face. The clerk flinched, dropped the magazine.

"Easy does it," I said to Elbow.

I looked around, conscious of other people. This was a college town that sat on the border of Iowa/Minnesota. My friends shopped at a food co-op and voted Obama. I wanted to avoid seeing anyone I knew for fear of what Elbow might say. On the way over, he'd asked what I did.

"You mean for a job?" I'd said.

"That's right," Elbow said.

"I'm working for a branch of the AmeriCorps," I said. "The Energy District. We retrofit homes so they're more efficient."

"You mean you work with silver-spoon do-gooders, prancing around old-ass homes caulking windows and sealing air-strips around doors." He hit me on the shoulder. "A feel-good project."

I looked out the window. It was that time of year when the mounds of snow were brown, receding, melting into the gutters, and the sun put forth more effort, guiding us into spring.

"Something like that," I said.

● ● ●

Elbow continued to stare at the clerk, straight faced, frustrated.

"Dude," the clerk said.

"Don't worry," Elbow said. "If I was gonna punch you, it would've happened."

"Wonderful," the clerk said.

"Look alive," Elbow said, shadowboxing around the clerk.

Elbow led me to the toy section where he grabbed a plas-

tic Uzi and handgun for our six-year-old nephew. He inspected each like he might inspect his own military issued M-16—
with meticulous detail and care. "Fucking sweet," he said,
holding them up. His eyes were focused and determined. I
was bored and craved something to snack on.

"I might need a Big Mac," I said. There was a McDonald's
attached to the Walmart.

"You shouldn't eat that," Elbow said. "Shit'll rot your
stomach."

"Getting hungry," I said. "Let's stop somewhere on the
way back."

"Hungry?" he said. "God, you civilians are weak. Talk to
me about hunger when you haven't eaten for four days." He
mumbled something else under his breath.

"What was that?"

"Fucking pussy," he said. He swung his cart toward my
thighs.

"Me?"

"Never mind," he said. He shook his head. "It's been a
rough few weeks." His face scrunched together, turned red.
He moved his cart away from me, down the aisle toward
checkout.

●　●　●

By the time we got back, the party was pretty much over. Elbow darted around the living room with our nephew, Jack,
son of two lawyers. They rolled their eyes at Elbow's gifts.

Jack held the Uzi proudly, aiming at every man, woman,
and child who entered his sights. Elbow armed himself with
the pistol. Together they formed a team—two Marines. They
took cover behind furniture and shot at imaginary enemies,
making gunfire sounds. Elbow shouted instructions to Jack.
"Cover me while I crawl to the piano."

"Got it," Jack said. Jack pointed his Uzi and started unloading. I was in the kitchen with the other adults, forking into dense, flourless cake, and wishing I could play alongside these guys without worrying about what the others thought. I wondered what Elbow would think of this dessert.

"Good shooting, Private," Elbow said, nodding affirmatively.

I sipped coffee. They were closing in on the kitchen, ready to take us hostage.

"Jack," Elbow said. "When I say 'attack,' make your move—I've got you covered. Roger, that?"

"Roger that," Jack said.

Elbow motioned his pistol in our direction. "Attack!"

Jack stormed the kitchen and started blasting at everything. As promised, Elbow covered him, sending bullets through all of us, yelling, "Die motherfuckers!" Jack grinned, looking pleased.

He pointed the Uzi at my chest and said to Elbow, "I'm taking this one hostage."

"He'll be useless to us," Elbow said. "Might as well do the deed right now."

I pleaded my case. "I'll be useful to you," I said. "I'll cooperate fully. I'll fight the good fight." They looked at each other to decide my fate. Their sneers told of my chances. Their confidence in me was miniscule, smaller than the distance between Jack's finger and the trigger.

BURROWING ANIMALS

Living out of my car wasn't working well because at night I was getting cramps and bedsores and couldn't fall into REM sleep, so I'd wake up with bags under my eyes, which in turn was preventing me from landing a job. I needed a job. My money was gone, and the only meals I could come by came from grocery store food samples. I'd walk around the store twice, eating cheese and cold cuts and sliced up fruit and talking sweet to moms who wore fancy clothes and make-up, carting around toddlers, and making eyes at the men who worked the meat counter. This lasted a month before I called my parents. I hadn't talked to them for almost as long as I hadn't talked to my own kids. When I called, my mom started sobbing. Then she handed the phone to my dad.

"When are you going to be here?" he said.

"I was hoping as soon as possible," I said. "Things are getting kind of rough."

"Rough?" he said. "Jesus Christ. I slept in a jungle in Nam, gooks hiding out in trees waiting to blow your fucking head off. What've you got? Couple aches and pains?"

Moving home was the last thing I wanted, but being home-less for a month threatened my sobriety and stability. I'd lost my apartment six months ago after my buddy's batch of meth blew up and set fire to the place. I'd been on my own or bouncing around friends' basements ever since.

I'd never felt more vulnerable to relapse than when I was

on my own and bored, without anyone to talk to, or be with. The grocery stores helped. And the weather. It was late May and everything had turned green and hopeful.

My mother was glad to have me home. She showed me my old room, which had been converted into storage—books and military equipment, a sewing machine, two dusty dressers, and a cot in the corner with a sleeping bag rolled out on top. "We can get you set up later," my mom said. "How about something to eat?"

"Not yet," my dad said. He stood behind her. He insisted he show me something. He had let me move back in on the condition that I help him trap some rodent that had burrowed under his woodpile. The woodpile was situated in the side yard—large pieces of tree trunk that he had yet to split for fire wood. I'd helped him chainsaw the downed trees two winters ago and piled it up.

Apparently he'd hired someone to fill in the hole and run a live trap, but nothing worked. On the phone, he'd said, "I'm going to need your help." And that was the first time I remember him requesting something of me—my actual help.

"It's probably a woodchuck," I said, staring at the wide burrow. It was dug straight down and angled under the woodpile. Fresh brown dirt spilled out from the hole. No tracks or signs of movement.

"The hell it is," my dad said. He walked over, but wouldn't look at the burrow.

"Look at it," I said. "It's probably a woodchuck."

"I'm not looking."

"What's your problem?" I said. "Just take a look."

When he got to the camper, twenty feet from the woodpile, he turned around. My dad was medium-sized with no special characteristics. He wore jeans and his arms hung at his sides. At that moment he seemed distant, like he was recalling some memory. Then he took off his baseball cap and rubbed his bald spot. "Here's the deal," he said. "You knew I was the smallest man on our crew in Nam?"

"Yeah, you told me."

"But I was also fearless and agile so they designated me as Tunnel Rat." He was talking to the ground. "Viet Cong had elaborate tunnels and underground hideouts, and I'd crawl into those burrows where there were poisonous spiders and ants, booby traps, scorpions. Sometimes humans." He set his hands on his head. A truck rumbled by, interrupting his thoughts. "Anyway," he said, looking back at me, "it's not a woodchuck—they're messy and careless." He put his ball cap back on. "Just trap the damn animal, and cover the hole."

●　　●　　●

My parents lived on the edge of Cedar Rapids in an older neighborhood that would've been considered country living ten years ago, but the city was sprawling south, toward Iowa City, and their neighborhood of old houses was surrounded by cul-de-sacs lined with two-story homes, big prominent garages, and short, immature trees staked in strategic places in the sodded yards. My parents went to bed early so at night I'd walk the quiet streets and look into the houses. There were no sidewalks, and the curbs were slightly angled, bridging the street and the yards, which were littered with plastic play toys and tipped over bikes. Sometimes I'd stand in the dark, between the streetlights, and watch parents move around the upstairs bedrooms. I imagined them pulling thin books off of shelves and reading to their kids, and kissing them on the forehead, and while it was something I longed for, I could never reconcile their lifestyle with my own. Even if I were rich and could've afforded to live there, I wouldn't have. I've always been both envious and radically put-off by those who can just simply be—those people who work, live, have kids, pay their bills, and go on like everything they have is some blessing, everything is just fine. Life is just fine. The world is just fine. That's not how it worked for me. Then again, nothing else was working for me either. I couldn't seem to get out of that perpetual state of: *I'm about to do something better with my life.*

When I got home from my walk that night, I went out to the woodpile. My mom kept a lawn chair in the side yard and I sat down and smoked a cigarette. I had two left and had been saving them for a moment just like this. I tilted my head back and watched the sky. Hardly any moon, so the stars popped. Satellites crossed one end to the other. A few shooting stars. I'd been at a planetarium once with my kids. It was shaped like an igloo, and once you got inside, they turned off all the lights and we rested on the ground, the kids' heads on each of my shoulders, and some guy with a nasal voice and a red-dot laser moved us around the sky, pointing out the constellations, their names and mythologies. Sitting on my mom's lawn chair, I couldn't remember any of it, just that it was the last good time I remember having with my kids.

I snubbed out my cigarette and got up from the chair, and was about to head inside, when the lilacs along the edge of the property began to rustle. I wished like hell that I'd been carrying a flashlight. I worked up the courage and tip-toed over. I couldn't see anything, and whatever had shaken the bushes had either run away or was using that fucked up animal logic: if I don't move, no one will see me—which might work in the dark but probably not any other time. Unless you're a fawn. Or an owl.

I checked the foothold trap. The iron clamp, the jaw, was smashed together, but the trap was empty. I leaned in to examine the dirt. No tracks. I inspected the trap. No fur. I pulled on the trap's chain which was tethered to a metal stake. It felt secure. I reset the trap, stepping on the handle and opening the jaws. I set the trigger just right. I lifted my hands slowly and then eased my foot off the handle and the trap stayed in place, just outside the hole.

●　　●　　●

My dad was ambitious about finding me a job. He worked as a floor manager at Gander Mountain, and my mom volunteered as a correctional officer, and mornings I'd wake up late and find the house empty and the newspaper opened to the classifieds, a yellow highlighter lying next to it on the table. There'd be a few jobs highlighted and I'd look around for a few more and send out applications. My dad had established a system for me to follow. He thought I was a decent guy, but he knew I couldn't get shit done on my own. He'd helped me write up a resume and made a hundred copies of it at work. He bought a box of envelopes and a roll of stamps. My job was to stuff the envelopes or, better yet, drive over to Office Max or Best Buy or wherever it was, and hand a manager my resume. My dad said it would show "good initiative." We even practiced my handshake.

I was getting into my car, ready to deliver my resume to various business owners, when I decided to check on the trap. It was a great day—full of spring renewal and life and the smell of damp air. I could've spent the rest of my life in that moment, but I'd agreed to other things, like trapping a burrowing animal, and searching for a job.

Some of the logs on one side—the side closest to the house—had tumbled in the yard. I picked them up, set them back on the pile, and then checked the trap which had been set off. A crow's foot lay inside the trap. The bird must've stepped directly onto the trigger and the jaws snapped and cut its foot clean-off. I picked it up and examined it—black, with rough ridges, and four sharp talons. No blood.

At dinner that night, my dad congratulated me on getting apps out to hiring businesses and my mom informed me that my kids would be coming over the next day.

"I had no idea," I said. "That's great."

For a while, things had been rough between me and my ex, and she didn't trust me with the kids. Considering my habits and excesses, I didn't trust me entirely with the kids either. So early on we'd agreed to unofficially give my custody rights to my parents so that they could see them on occasional Wednesdays and every other weekend. "But," my mom said, "it's under the condition that if you were here, I'd tell her."

"I haven't seen them in over a year," I said.

"That's your own damn fault," my dad said.

"Thomas," my mother said, slapping the table. We were eating meatloaf and potatoes and green beans. Friday evening tradition. My dad sipped an Old Style. "For this first time," my mom said, looking at me, "I think it'd be best if you stayed elsewhere. It's just the one night."

I put my napkin on the table and leaned close to her. "Mom, look, I understand, but just let me see them for chrissake."

"Easy on the language," my dad said. Pieces of meatloaf flew out of his mouth.

"Please pass the green beans," I said.

"If those kids tell their mother, then we"—she pointed at herself and my dad—"we will lose our privileges. I'm not going to risk that."

●　　●　　●

That evening I strolled around the cul-de-sacs. Most lights were off, people sleeping, but there were occasional houses lit up, people watching late night news or a sitcom. The air felt cool and fresh. I slipped my hands into my pockets and kept walking, and when one street would dead-end, instead of turning around, I'd cut through empty, unsold lots over to the next street and look through the tunnel of connecting backyards. My kids lived in a neighborhood like this one, somewhere on the west side of town, and as much as I hated these subdivisions, I knew I could never provide for them like their mom and stepfather.

I moved down the street, slipping past darkened cars and stopping every once in a while to watch a couple on the couch, drinking wine, watching television. There was no great interest in this for me, just something to do. A little further ahead I came upon a car parked on the side of the road with its interior lights on. When I was a kid, out with my dad, he'd reach into the stranger's lit-up car and flip off the light. "Prevent a dead battery. Our good deed for the day," he'd say. I opened the driver's side door and reached up to click-off the dome light. As I was reaching, I heard a door open and shut, and some guy came out of the house.

"What the—" he pulled a cell phone off his belt and started dialing.

"The light was on," I said. "I was turning it—"

"Bullshit," he said. "Yeah," he said into the phone, "I got some guy breaking into my car, he's standing right in front of me."

I didn't even think about it, I just started sprinting, directly away from the house, across the street, through side-yards, backyards, I hurdled a couple picket fences, dashed through to the other streets, and when I finally reached the stretch of trees that divided my parents' neighborhood from the new developments, I stopped. I looked back. No one. I put my hands on my knees and caught my breath.

Saturday, breakfast. My dad poured me a coffee and, like I was in high school, handed me the sports section. I liked keeping track of the baseball stats. The rest of the paper lay out in front of him and my mom. He liked reading the op-eds. My mother was hiding out behind the Iowa Today section. I sipped coffee. "I think it's a badger," I said.

My dad looked different in his reading glasses. "A badger?" my mom asked. "We don't have those around here, do we, Thomas?"

"Hard to say," my dad said.

"They're neat freaks. And paranoid," I said. "They crawl into their holes backward so they can spot anything stalking them. I read about it online."

"Here you go," my dad said. He handed me the classifieds. "I'd rather not talk about the trap right now. Breakfast is meant to be peaceful."

●　　●　　●

My mom had made me a bed in the camper. She even packed a few peanut butter sandwiches, chips, a bag of washed grapes, and a few jugs of water.

My wife dropped off my son and daughter at three in the afternoon. With no kids for the night, I'm sure she was looking forward to her evening. When we were together and our kids were 1 and 3, my parents would babysit for a night and ask about our "big plans," and we'd tell them we were going for dinner and a movie, but instead we'd just go home and have the place to ourselves—sitting around in our underwear, watching movies, making love on the couch, eating out of to-go containers, empty beer and wine bottles strewn throughout the house. We loved our kids, but twenty-four hours of freedom never felt better.

From inside the camper, I watched my kids slide out the backseat of a white Suburban and my legs almost gave out. I'd been sober for a while now, and as difficult as it had been at some points, this made it worth it. My ex and my mom talked in the driveway while my dad hugged the kids. My boy, the youngest, was holding a paper airplane, guiding it through the air. He was eight, my daughter was ten. Her hair was pulled back into a ponytail. The backpack she wore probably held their pajamas, slippers, and toothbrushes. She looked exactly like her mother—slender, long-limbed, a generous smile. Her features were kind and thoughtful and intelligent, and I could already imagine all the good she'd contribute to the world as a way to make up for what I couldn't do. My son ran over to the swing set—an old rusted metal contraption that my dad had put together the day our daughter was born. My son pumped his legs and got going on the swing, his paper airplane lying in the dirt. My ex-wife hugged my mother, got back in her Suburban and pulled away. I stared at my kids, tried flipping open the camper door handle. I tried to push it open. Then I started really pushing. It had been padlocked from the outside. My dad waved to me as he motioned for the kids to go inside.

"Couldn't take any chances," my dad said. He opened the lock. It was about eight at night, dark out, kids' bedtime. I stepped out and breathed in the fresh air. I pulled the last cigarette out of the pocket of my flannel. I sparked the lighter and took a drag.

"You'd have been the first to die in Nam," my dad said.

"The fuck are you talking about?" I took a drag, and tried not to look at him.

"Oh, settle down," he said. "It's your own damn fault you got locked in. I knew you'd try to come out. You were always the most predictable out of you and your brothers. When you were 10 years old, I told your mother you were a coin toss. A fifty-fifty. Even that was generous."

"I don't get it."

"Whether you'd make it or not," he said. "I told her you were gonna get your ass in trouble—with drugs, the law—and sure enough. She was in denial, you were her baby." We stood there in silence, the clear night sky, the smell of spring air.

After a minute, he said, "You were just a little too squirrely."

I sucked hard on the cigarette and coughed. I hadn't been smoking much at all, and the nicotine hit me hard. I wanted to say something to defend myself, but I didn't want to fight. And all the evidence was on his side.

"Vietcong snipers used to scope Americans in the jungle at night," my dad said. "It was so dark in those jungles, you might as well have been blindfolded. Anyway, they'd find cigarette cherries in the dark, aim right for them. Guys getting shot in the face and throat, no one could figure it out. Until they figured it out." He stuck his hand in my face. "Give me a quick puff." I passed him the cigarette. "Your mother likes having you around," he said, exhaling smoke through his nose and mouth. He used to smoke a pipe, but hadn't for a while. "But she's concerned." He passed it back, and tried to blow a smoke ring.

"She's gonna smell that smoke on you," I said.

"No," he said. "She won't."

"You and mom sleeping in different rooms again?"

● ● ●

I went to the windows and watched my kids reading under table lamps that sat next to each bed. My daughter was reading *Holes*, a book I'd never heard of but it had that silver award patch in the lower right corner of the cover so I figured it was good, and my son was reading a book about giants—a book I used to read when I was his age.

Pretty soon, my dad entered the room and said, "Lights out," and they turned off their lamps and tucked themselves in. I wished like hell I could say goodnight to them, but that wasn't part of the plan.

After that, I tried eating in the camper, but I had no appetite. I crumbled up part of a peanut butter sandwich and went outside and sprinkled the crumbs around the trap, and then

I went inside and made a call to a woman I'd known from another life. I needed someone around, some company. Her name was Tammy and we'd met at AA, and she was always decent to talk to.

● ● ●

First thing she did when she stepped into the camper was unroll a Ziploc sandwich baggie holding one skinny joint.

"It's tough to have sex when I'm not drunk or high, and I'm working hard to stay off the booze," she said. She sat down at the edge of the bed and lit the joint, puffed twice, and passed it to me. I'd been booze and drug free for so long, but this didn't seem too harmful, contained in just this camper.

After we smoked I pulled the window shut and she undressed and got under the covers. I was surprised any of this was actually happening, but she acted like it was the most normal thing in the world. When we were finished, I felt this great surge of energy and wanted to talk about our future lives—not ours together, but just generally speaking. She rolled away from me and reached for her clothes.

"If you were more interesting, I'd consider staying and chatting," she said. And just like that, the conversation was over. I sat up and looked around for my underwear and pants. I rolled off the bed. Then she said, "You were always too damn sappy and talked too much in meetings—talking about your kids and shit. You just need to make shit happen for yourself and stop talking so much."

Tammy patted me on the shoulder and left, and I stayed up trying to read *Harry Potter*, book one. My daughter had sped through the entire series and I thought if I could get through at least one, we might have something to talk about. At the end of page two, I heard a loud snap and then a screech.

I jumped up, put my clothes on, strapped on a headlamp, and stepped out of the camper. I could hear a hissing, and the chain on the trap snapping tight. In the light, I saw two glow-ing eyes. Whatever it was, it struggled to get out. Its claws pawed at the earth, a low-grumbling hiss.

The trap hadn't done too much damage to the cat. "Jesus, goddamn," I said. "This isn't your den." It wouldn't stop hiss-ing at me, and it had peed in the dirt. It smelled horrible. I stood there for a minute trying to figure out what to do—how to release it without being attacked. I hated this trap.

I inched closer and the cat held a front paw in the air, its claws coming out. I backed away. I grabbed a long piece of firewood, and kept a light on the cat. It was black and white and mangy, still pawing at the air, and trying to pull away. I set the log down on the spring. The jaws opened just enough for the cat to pull free. It darted off into the bushes without issue.

I decided not to mention the stray to my dad. He would've gotten worked up about it, and I didn't need him worrying. The trap had been reset, but instead of keeping it on the ground I set it in between a few logs with a half of a peanut butter sandwich behind it so that whatever reached in to grab the sandwich would get its forepaw caught. I still wasn't even sure what the big deal was, but my dad had it in his head that whatever was burrowing in there needed to be gone. He could hardly stand to be near the camper, let alone the actual woodpile.

● ● ●

My ex picked up the kids at 3 p.m. that Sunday. I watched from the camper as my kids walked from the house to the Suburban, giving their mother enthusiastic hugs, and piling in the back. After they left, my mom said, "Next time I'll work out something so that you can see them. Next time."

With my kids gone, I couldn't imagine myself being around my parents. I couldn't sit at a table with them and eat leftovers and talk about what it would be like when the kids came over next Wednesday. I couldn't do it. I knew they'd have a lot to say—advice to give—and I couldn't hear that either. I locked the camper and stayed in there another night.

But I couldn't sleep. Couldn't even relax. At around 4 in the morning, I left for the new developments. I'd noted an open garage door the last few times on my walks, an observation leftover from my days as a thief. I could pass by an open garage and assess the risk of entering and the street value of everything in there in a matter of seconds. You look for small valuables, things that are easy to transport, carry, things that would fit into a car or van without taking up too much space. The garage I'd marked had power tools, a pair of mountain bikes, a rack of fall/winter jackets, and golf clubs. Other things: posters of women in bikinis, a work bench that appeared new, a full size fridge, and a few yard games. Back in the day, I'd have no issue stealing from someone like this: no kids, careless, ungrateful, makes too much money.

At first I strolled past the house. The garage door had been shut. I checked the side door. It was open. I stepped inside. It smelled damp, the slight residue of gas. I peered into the cars—a Grand Cherokee and a Volvo—and they were both clean, empty. I opened the fridge and took out two cans of beer.

I valued the garage at five-six hundred dollars, with most of the money coming from the power tools and the bikes. I was glad those days were over. I took the set of golf clubs and a bucket of balls that sat on the concrete slab next to the golf bag. I cracked one of the beers and tip-toed out the door.

● ● ●

My grandfather was a sheet-metal worker and hadn't started golfing until he turned sixty-five. After that he mostly hit balls at the shooting range or tooled around three-par golf courses, lugging his garage-sale golf clubs. Mostly, I think he liked walking around outside—the fresh air, the birds. He never kept score or knew what his handicap was.

After twenty years, I still remembered what he taught me. My shoulders were a little tight and it made it difficult to swing, but after I hit a few, I loosened up. I stretched. It felt good to be out there at night, slightly buzzed after just one beer. It wasn't even as good as I thought it was going to taste, but I opened the other anyway and threw the empty in the dirt. I stood at the edge of one of the neighborhoods where, during the day, you could see a cow pasture a half-mile away. At night you could smell the pungent odor of cow manure, and you could almost hear them chewing on grass, lowing in the field.

I smacked golf balls into the dark. I swung as hard as I could. I had no idea where they were landing, but I knew they were hitting more dirt—open land that was getting sized-up for subdivision. I wasn't even coming close to the cows. They were safe.

I teed off until the bucket was empty and after I was finished I lugged the bag of golf clubs down the street, set it in front of its owner's house, and headed home. The sun was just starting to crack the eastern sky, a line of orange, the clouds above the horizon reflected pink.

●　●　●

"Jesus Christ, wake up." My dad was slapping the side of the camper. I stepped out, groggy. He took me by the shoulder and pointed at the woodpile. A badger—brown and gray and black with a white stripe that ran from its nose to its tail—its front paw caught in the trap. It was scratching the dirt, pulling on the chain. The animal itself made no noise. It knew we were there, but it didn't stop pulling and for as long as we watched, it didn't make a sound. My dad was holding a shovel.

"I can't believe it's a badger," I said. I rubbed my face and eyes. "They're rare, aren't they?"

"They're nocturnal," he said. "They're not rare, just a rare sight." He handed me the shovel. "Can't shoot a gun in city limits."

"You want me to kill it with this?" I held the shovel away from myself. "Aren't you supposed to be at work?" It was a bright sunny morning.

"A couple good thwacks should do it," he said.

I shuffled over to the badger. It smelled awful, like a skunk. The claws were scurrying at the dirt, frantically, but not going anywhere. The trap was well staked. I looked at the hearty foot. The trap caught the badger high on the well-padded forepaw. No visible blood.

"If I let this thing go, it'll live," I said. "It'll be fine. Its foot is fine."

"I don't want that thing making burrows and underground hideouts around this woodpile," he said. "Too close to the house. Too close for comfort."

"It won't come back after this—they're paranoid."

"You're crazy if you think I'm taking that risk."

He grabbed the shovel from me. He brought the shovel up over his head and the badger turned its face toward him. A proud gesture. My dad hesitated, the shovel hanging in the air. I turned around and observed the row of lilacs along the border between my parents' house and the neighbors. The flowers had just bloomed—violet and fragrant.

I can't really describe the sound of the shovel meeting the badger's skull. But it did, twice, and when I turned around to look my dad was walking away. "I can't finish it off," he said. The badger lay on its side, paws slowly scraping the air, syrupy blood dripping out of its mouth and nose. It groaned and hissed at the same time. The shovel lay where my dad had stood.

There was no time to think. I picked up the shovel and swung: once, twice, three times. I lowered the shovel and felt myself breathing heavy, my heart racing, pounding, like I'd just run a race. I'd read later that their skulls are thick and robust, and while this made sense, it didn't make me feel any better for how many times we'd struck the badger. When I was a kid, I shot one sparrow with my bb gun. I hated myself for it—made me want to puke.

I turned away from the badger and lifted the shovel high over my head and brought the handle down hard over my thigh. It split in two so that I was holding separate pieces. I threw the wooden handle into the lilac bushes and threw the other part onto the ground. My dad picked up the discarded and started rinsing off the blade.

"Goddamn it," I said.

"I can't have something burrowing in my yard," my dad said, staring hard at the nozzle of the hose. "It's a hazard, a nuisance. For me, for everyone."

"You think that thing would've attacked you?" I moved toward the badger. I nudged it with my foot. It was a heap of flesh and bones, gone. "That's the dumbest thing I've ever heard."

"Settle down," my dad said. I turned away from him. He finished rinsing the blood off the shovel. He walked up behind me and set a hand on my shoulder.

"Don't," I said.

"Get over yourself," he said. "You kill a badger, and I'm unloading my military issued .45 on people inside those tunnels in Nam. My guys would hear me blasting away, and they'd rush to pull me out of the hole, my ears ringing like church bells."

My dad went back in the house. I unlatched the badger's foot from the jaws of the trap and unstaked the chain. The area around the burrow, once a clean, smooth dirt surface, was now torn up and messy. I found another shovel and started digging a hole.

I worked up a sweat. I started feeling faint. Before I buried the badger I went in for a glass of orange juice. My parents had already left for work. My kids' artwork covered half the kitchen table and most of the fridge, their books and toys laid out in one corner of the living room floor.

The message machine was blinking, and, thinking it could be a manager wanting an interview, I clicked play. It was my ex. I stopped the message right away, not wanting to hear her voice, or what she had to say. I milled through the fridge and uncovered a plate of leftovers and smelled to see if it was still okay. I stuck it in the microwave. While the food was warming up, I went back and stood over the answering machine, pushed a button. "Thanks, Jean," she said, "for all the updates."

Her voice. Her clear, well-enunciated words. She sounded professional *and* sweet. Sincere *and* competent.

"I'd like to talk about him seeing the kids. I'm open to it, especially if it's at your house, but still, I'd like to talk. I have some concerns, as we've already discussed. But again, thank you for the update,"—and this is the part I could never understand—she said, "I'm so glad he's getting better."

Better? I wanted to dial her number, but I'd forgotten it. I wanted to dial her number and say, "Sweetheart, better? Have you seen me lately?" I wanted to invite her over. "Come see me, darling," I'd say. "Come see what I'm capable of."

COMPANY
&
COMPANIONSHIP

I called her Georgia because she was from Georgia. I don't remember her real name, and not so sure if I ever knew. She was sent to me by an ill-advised friend who told her I was trustworthy and could help her out, which is to say, rent her a room. Georgia had a restraining order on two different men who finally came together with the common purpose of killing her, or so she informed our mutual friend who consequently told me. I had a rental house off Tenth Street, sandwiched between two well-meaning families, so the first thing I told Georgia was this: don't invite anyone over, don't make phone calls from this house, and don't eat any of my cereal. She responded with a head nod. She could eat anything else except the cereal. Cereal prices were outrageous.

I know you're curious, so I'll tell you right now: she was blond with hair combed straight back to her neckline, tan skin and brown eyes, and if you'd given her a surfboard she'd look like a model for *Outside Magazine*. She was originally from here, from Iowa, which explains why she didn't have a southern accent, but at times—more times than I care to admit—I imagined her with a deep scarlet drawl.

She showed no desire to interact with me on any level. Trust me. I tried to get her to do a lot of things, none of which she obliged, talking included. Still, the company was something I needed. Even just having someone around, another body in this old, lonely house, kept my mind sharp. Kept me from plummeting.

I owed our mutual friend, Suzy, something close to my actual life so it was never a hesitation to allow Georgia a room. She paid rent, which I didn't ask for, one hundred dollars every four or five weeks. The house had a huge living room with tall ceilings and fir floors. It was a rundown turn-of-the-century Queen Anne, but in a decent neighborhood. I had originally sub-let a room from a couple who'd since split up. After they left, I just stuck around and paid the landlord what I could. I don't think he ever knew what was going on.

I'd arranged a couch in the middle of the living room, and one night I rented a movie, and Georgia and I watched it together, both of us sitting on either end of the couch. I paused in the middle of the movie.

"Would you like popcorn?" I said. "I like popcorn with my movies."

Nothing, not a word.

"I'm not opposed to other snacks," I said. "I could make us some nachos or mini tacos, something easy like that."

She picked up *Us Weekly*, one of her magazines, and started thumbing through.

I touched her bare thigh to see what she thought of that, and she didn't move. Just sat there rigid and seemingly content. Her skin was smooth and warm, and I felt something in myself that I hadn't felt in a while. Just touching another human being, sexual or not, brought on some arousal of the spirit.

"You know," I said. "You remind me of someone. When I think of who, I'll let you know."

The next weekend, I brought over a friend named McDowell, a former pastor turned queer, which is to say he'd always been gay but finally came out. He liked to smoke pot and snort the occasional line, but that was all. Stayed away from everything else. I liked him. He was a good listener, which was a skill he'd learned as a pastor. He told me once that he'd hated almost everyone in his congregation, and he also told me that pretty much every pastor loves the power-trip of pastoring more than God, which sounded as true of a statement as I'd ever heard from a pastor. Anyway, I invited him over one night, my first guest since Georgia had moved in. I prepped McDowell for all of it, told him she doesn't talk, etc. etc., but also told him she was a world-class knockout, and joked that I'd planned a honeymoon for us that she wasn't aware of, so I asked him to keep that to himself. And like any good pastor, he could keep a secret. I trusted McDowell's judgment on just about everything more so than I trusted my own. So I asked him to help crack the code with Georgia.

He brought over a bag of microwaveable pizza pockets, and that's what I made for dinner. McDowell cut lines of candy on a paper plate and snorted. He offered some to Georgia, and she accepted. After that, she was in a mood I'd never seen before—her shoulders relaxed and I think she even smiled. It was all for the better. I warmed up all six hot pockets, two for everyone in the house, but Georgia didn't bother. After those lines, she was back on the couch with her legs tucked under so that she was sitting on her feet, holding that same *Us Weekly*.

"I'm McDowell," he said. He held out his hand. Everything was happening backwards. First the coke, then the introductions. I'd already taken two lines in the kitchen, and my mind felt clean and pure. McDowell stretched out his hand in the gentle way of pastors. She just looked at him. He offered to fork-feed her a pizza pocket, and she actually smiled.

"You'd do that?" she said.

What was it with women and gay men? And why hadn't I thought of fork-feeding her?

McDowell cut up the veggie pizza pocket, steam curled into the air. He blew on each piece before setting the fork into her mouth, as gentle as a robin feeding its young. I watched with what you might call envy *and* disbelief.

By the end of the night, we were all sufficiently drunk and high, except they were on the couch, hip-to-hip, laughing and drinking bottled beer, the fancy kind that I'd bought for an occasion such as this. I was stuck on the recliner trying to find a way into their conversation.

McDowell had just finished a story about one of his ex-lovers who he had been with prior to leaving the church, about how they did it in his church office, and how at the time he felt horrible guilt, but now he loves talking about it. Georgia kept asking him about his love life. And that's when I thought about my own. I considered that maybe my biggest downfall in relationships is that I put all my interest in one person, neglecting friends and family members, and now that I was out of a relationship I had the most difficult time meeting people. It takes forever to get to know someone, and half the people I ran around with were here one minute, gone the next.

There was a lull in their conversation. "You guys wanna hit the bars?" I said.

Georgia held up her St. Pauli Girl. "Do you have any more of these?"

"So, no bar?"

"I could use another one too," McDowell said. Together they took up one cushion.

As I walked toward the kitchen, I heard McDowell say to Georgia, "You should consider moving in with me, we'd have a ball together."

●　●　●

On the phone with McDowell, several days later, he suggested that in fact we might move Georgia from house to house to keep the conspirators off her back.

"They're more than likely still in the south," I said.

"But she's from here, right?"

"True," I said.

"Present her with the idea," he said.

"If she moves in with you, will you invite me over?" I said.

"Maybe," he said. "It'd be so nice for a little company and companionship. I'm at that point in my life where a room-mate could be nice."

"You wanna sleep with her, don't you?" I said. "You're not supposed to want that."

"Who are you to say?" he said. I could tell he was disgusted.

"I don't know anything anymore," I said. There was a brief pause. Then, "Can you please not ask her to your home?"

"You're testing my patience," he said. "And no, for your information, I don't want to sleep with her. More like cuddle. We could just share the same bed. That would be okay with me."

Weeks went by and Georgia stuck around. McDowell found himself some other love interest, some other company and companionship, and our friendship faded as did his interest in Georgia. Our lives were like that. One minute it was *this*, the next it was *that*. I didn't know anyone with a sustained interest in anything. Sometimes it all felt like a waste of time.

The summer was closing quickly, and I thought it important that Georgia get outside with more frequency as not to develop a vitamin D deficiency, which was a hot topic for sunscreen users and moms wading around the toddler pool at Daniel's Park, the one I hung around in the afternoons to cool off. No admission fee.

"That's a nice offer," Georgia said. She'd been talking more since McDowell's visit. Still, we weren't what you'd call *close*.

"I'll pack us a snack and we can go to the free pool at the park."

"It's time for me to move on," she said. That was when I noticed a tote bag sitting at her feet. She was standing in the living room next to the couch. She was holding a brand new *Us Weekly*. The cover photo was a celeb couple that I sort of recognized. They had their arms around each other, amongst a crowd of people, smiling. They looked drunk and happy.

"I feel like you just got here," I said. "Like we're just getting to know each other. I'd prefer if you stayed another night or two on account of those restraining orders, I hear those two guys are getting close."

"I have no idea what you're talking about."

"Your two ex-boyfriends who joined together. It's unfortunate, I'm really sorry you have to go through all that."

"Is that what Suzy said?" She laughed. I'd known Suzy forever. She used to have a meth problem.

"She said it was a secret, not to tell anyone," I said. "I haven't told anyone. Well, just McDowell, but he's a pastor."

"There's no restraining order," she said. "I just needed a place to crash for a few months."

"No restraining order?"

"Is that a problem?"

"I just—"

"I get it," she said. "You thought you were doing me some huge favor by protecting me."

"I thought—"

"I used to work for Suzy's live-in boyfriend," she said. "He was a sleaze, tried to feel me up at work, and I put him in the hospital. That's why I couldn't stay with her."

"No shit?"

"Shattered his nose, bruised his balls."

"Nice."

"That happened forever ago, but you know what they say: people don't change."

"Do you think that's true?" I said.

"Suzy and I are still friends, despite what happened," she said, as a way to prove her point.

I carried her luggage out to the curb. It was a Sunday, I

think, and the neighbor kids were playing on plastic toys in their front yards and the dads were standing nearby in khaki shorts and collared shirts, looking ready for a game of golf. I never really adjusted fully to that neighborhood. Never felt like I fit in.

"Could we maybe just talk about this," I said. "This seems unnecessary."

She touched my elbow, and said my name three times. The cab pulled up a few seconds later. Georgia didn't say a word, just got into the backseat and pulled away.

"Well to hell with you anyway!"

Walking back to the house, I waved to my neighbors. They gave me quizzical, sympathetic looks.

"Relational issues," I said.

They gave a half-hearted chuckle, raised their beers, and refocused on whatever they'd been discussing previously.

Later, and this was the part that made me think differently of her, I was cleaning in the kitchen, rearranging things. I opened the pantry and there, inside, were three new boxes of Lucky Charms that she must've bought and stocked while I was out of the house. And later still, I dialed McDowell and told him the story. He sniffed into the phone. He had that nasally congestion that came instantly after a bump, and I swear, to this day, I heard a woman's voice in the background. But why would I inquire? What would it matter anyhow?

A month went by before I saw Suzy at the Red Frog with a guy who I thought might be the sleaze boyfriend Georgia told me about. I got really close to him, inspecting his nose, and sure enough, it was altered in the way broken noses have been altered. Slightly off kilter, a bulge in an unlikely place. I got close, and stared for a minute too long.

"What the fuck?" he said, leaning away from me.

"What's Georgia feel like?"

"Who the fuck are you?" he said. He had a confused, scared look on his face which gave me a feeling of invincibility, like I had all the control. Suzy was at the other end of the bar in cut-offs and a t-shirt, looking good.

"Friends with Suzy," I said. "That's all."

"Friends, huh?" he said. He had the self-esteem of a beaten puppy. How could you hate a man like that? I felt sorry for the guy.

"I've known her since grade school," I said. "We were neighbors."

I've never told anyone this, but Suzy used to hold my hand while we walked past the old haunted house with the big dogs on our way to school. Every day for the entire second grade, she kept me safe. Later, in high school, I tried to fool around with her but she never liked me like that. I was hoping for another shot with her later that night.

I got drunk, as did everyone in the bar, and every face there reminded me of something sad. So I drank more, and we all swayed to music that no one listens to anymore. At some point, I whispered in Suzy's ear that I wanted to meet her out back in five minutes. I could feel her soft brown hair against my nose. I kissed her ear lobe to suggest what I wanted from her, and as the way of tunnel-vision drunks, no one in their state noticed what had happened. We parted ways, and I slipped outside with a Winston in my mouth and the pack in my hand.

The lights in the alley had been burnt out and never replaced. I found a spot somewhere behind the bar that would do just fine, and then Suzy came stumbling outside. I went to meet her so I could lead her back there. As she moved toward the end of the building, she tripped on a rain gutter. I caught her by the waist, found enough balance for both of us. I held her, brought her close. She laughed at her near folly, and I kept a strong hold of her, burying my face in her neck and kissing her here and there, and while this was happening, I thought of asking her about Georgia, and why she'd made up that story, but decided none of that mattered anymore because I was all-consumed by being this close to someone for the first time since I could remember, and as I continued to hold her, her body pressed against my own, something in me must've loosened. My legs almost gave out, and she must've sensed this because she held me tighter. And for a moment, I was frozen. Couldn't do anything, couldn't say anything. I just melted into her, and like she'd done so many times before, she took my hands into hers, leaned in to me. "You're gonna be all right," she said. "You're gonna be just fine."

BLOOD TRAIL

They stood at the edge of the forest, where it opened onto a strip of prairie grass. Just beyond the grass was a terraced cornfield, working its way upward to a gravel road about a quarter-mile away.

The snow had started around noon. Wet, heavy flakes. Eli raised his shotgun and brought the butt firm against his shoulder. He rested his cheek against the walnut stock and looked into the scope. "I can't make out any snowflakes," he said, lowering and raising his gun, trying to locate the flakes, first against the sky, and then the trees. "I can't dial in."

"You obviously need some work with that scope," his dad said. "The way you botched that shot."

It had been a long shot, around a hundred yards, and the only reason he'd taken it was because his dad could see the deer. Had he missed, Eli would not have cared, and they wouldn't be in the position of having to track a wounded animal.

The deer was, according to his dad, "a big mama doe, with tons of good meat on her." She'd walked the edge of the tree line before stopping, turning broadside, and then walking toward the cornfield. Two smaller deer had lagged behind. He wouldn't have had a closer shot so, sitting against a tree, he had rested the slug-gun on his knee, drawn in a deep breath, found the crosshairs in his scope, and set his sight on the deer's front quarters—heart and lung area. He followed the deer with the crosshairs: a fat, old deer, whose coat had turned a thick, rough winter brown. He'd let half his breath out, relaxed his arms, and squeezed the trigger. Just as his father had taught while using a pellet gun. He couldn't shoot without hearing his dad's words: "Squeeze the trigger. Don't pull, squeeze."

Blood had gushed at the initial area of contact. "Dark blood," his dad said. "Probably a brisket shot." His dad looked at him. "Not good for tracking. Won't be a ton of blood."

●　　●　　●

Now they would have to wait, let the deer run and settle in, and then start tracking.

"General rule," his dad said, "is an hour."

"I don't think we need to wait that long," Eli said.

His dad shook his head. "You didn't get a good shot. She took off pretty hard after you fired. She'll need a while to stiffen up."

They stood there for another minute, looking around, the snow collecting on their blaze orange vests and stocking caps. "Let's sit for a while," his dad said. "See if another one strolls through."

It was early December, the temperature just below freezing. The sky, a soft gray. They sat on either side of an oak tree. Eli watched squirrels scurry around in the newly settled snow, gathering and gnawing on nuts. The trees, bare. Their uppermost branches knuckling together in the breeze, creaking.

After a while, Eli dozed off, his shotgun resting on his legs. He woke up to the turn of his dad's thermos cap. His dad poured a cup of coffee, his back still resting against the tree, still scanning for movement in the woods. "I'll take some if you have more," Eli whispered. The smell of the coffee made him long for warmth and home. Eli had always liked the idea of hunting more than the hunting itself. The coffee served as a reminder of the lazy morning he'd wanted. He didn't want to be out here. And with every passing hour he had to remind himself that their hunting excursion happened only one weekend a year.

Eli stood while his father poured another cup. "Now don't get too ambitious," his dad said. "We'll slow-hunt for a while, walk nice and easy, see if we can nab another deer."

"We'll be tracking on someone else's property," Eli said. "We're supposed to unload our guns if we do that."

"Don't be an asshole," his dad said. "You see any houses? No one'll notice."

"They'll hear us if you shoot."

"Or if you shoot."

"I'm not shooting," Eli said. "I already have a deer."

"You don't have shit," his dad said. "Your goddamn deer is wounded."

His dad handed him a cup of coffee.

"What about the snow?" Eli said, after a sip.

"What about it?" his dad said.

"It'll be tough to track."

"The blood will show through," his dad said. "And the snow won't collect as well in the woods. That deer's bedded in there somewhere."

●   ●   ●

At first the tracking was easy. The deer had been on a dead sprint before ducking into the woods and disappearing into a steep ravine. Eli and his dad walked up to the barbed wire fence. He realized, then, that he'd shot it on someone else's property. Why didn't he notice this at the time he shot? The distance must've thrown him off. If his dad had noticed, he hadn't said anything.

●   ●   ●

They followed small drops of blood to the edge of the forest where the deer had disappeared, eraser-sized droplets every few feet. The woods on this property were dense. Buckthorn and briar patches caught against their Carhartt pants, sometimes going right through.

While Eli kept his shotgun slung over his shoulder, his dad kept his in the ready position: left hand on the forestock, right hand on the handle, finger on the trigger. His dad's was a semiautomatic slug gun. Black composite with open sights. He didn't have a rifled barrel like Eli's, but what he lost in accuracy, he gained in the number of shots—five total.

Eli had bought his single-shot because the saleswoman owned the same one and he thought this might impress her. But when he went to ask her out after making the purchase, she hemmed and hawed, and said, *it's not a good time*. Still, Eli liked the gun's distance and accuracy, and the scope. Until today, all the deer he'd shot had dropped upon impact. "I get neck shots," Eli had bragged to his friends. "They crumple and fold on the spot." And while this was sometimes true, he was never really proud of these confessions. It was just something he said while giving away venison neatly wrapped in white freezer paper, permanent marker scribbled on the outside to indicate the cut of meat. He could never eat the deer. Not after having shot it, and watching it writhe, its dying legs rustling up leaves or snow, its back buckling before the tongue goes limp, slipping out of its mouth. After that, Eli couldn't bear the thought of forking the flesh into his mouth.

Halfway down the ravine, five deer spooked and ran up the other side. Eli's dad shot three times. The report left Eli's ears ringing. "Fuck," his dad said. "I didn't see them 'til it was too late. Too far of a shot."

Tracking another deer, especially this far from the truck, would only have complicated their situation, so he was glad his father had missed. The two kept walking down the slope, at an angle, occasionally holding onto saplings to keep their balance.

The bottom of the ravine was quiet, still. Eli pointed to oval-shaped areas of leaves and twigs that had not been exposed to the snow. "Here's where they were bedding down."

"Do you still have the trail?" his dad said. "Any blood?"

"Barely," Eli said. "But she couldn't have gone much farther."

"They usually take the easiest path when they're injured," his dad said. "I'd be surprised if she ran back up the hill."

Down in the ravine there was less underbrush. More fallen trees, but this wasn't as bad as wading through thorn bushes. Eli trudged along next to his father, who was still hunting, searching ahead, scanning for any movement. After about a half mile, the blood had trickled to a small drop every ten feet or so.

His dad had been right. The deer hadn't moved uphill. She'd stayed on the bottom, bobbing and weaving her way through downed logs and brush. They paused for a minute while his dad tied his boot, then he reached into his vest pocket and pulled out a flask and a pack of Winstons. "Usually don't smoke or drink unless we're celebrating. But what the hell."

It would be getting dark soon and Eli wanted his dad to give up. Leave the deer. Come back and search in the morning. But even that idea wasn't appealing. To hell with the deer.

But despite his father's hunting infringements—trespassing, loaded guns on someone else's land—his dad would not stop searching for the wounded animal. Eli accepted a pull from the flask.

"Bushmills," his dad said. "Damn good, huh?"

"Not bad."

They lit cigarettes. "We might not be giving it enough time to bed down and stiffen up," his dad said.

"It hasn't bedded down, yet." Eli said. "We would've seen the spot."

"That's what I mean," his dad said.

"Maybe we should call it a day."

His father took another pull of whiskey. "And come back tomorrow?"

"I guess," Eli said.

"You guess?" his dad said. "I guess you don't want to help put food on the table. I guess someone else taught you how to hunt. You can't just give up." It was a comment his dad made every hunting season—"putting food on the table." Eli knew it was all bullshit. They weren't starving. They were never starving. His dad just liked to hunt.

"Fine," Eli said. "Let's come back tomorrow."

"No," his dad said. "We're gonna keep going."

They pushed along, climbing over logs, backing their way through thorn bushes, and came to an area that was completely open. "I bet it's a food plot," his dad said. "Look there." He pointed to what looked like a tree house perched on long wooden poles supported with two-by-sixes hammered into an X. "Whoever built this deer-stand is pretty serious about their hunting." His dad reached to the ground and picked at brown plants. It was a mixture of beans, sorghum, corn, and alfalfa.

They moved away from the food plot, and came to a dry creek bed. As Eli stepped down into it his father raised his gun and fired a shot. And fired again.

"Shit," his dad said. "Fucking deer surprised me."

"You hit it?" Eli said.

"I don't know," his dad said. "It kept running."

Eli stomped up and out of the creek bed and started hiking up the ravine. He wanted to show his frustration without getting into a yelling match, but halfway up the hill, he looked back to see about his dad, and found him walking up the hill in the opposite direction. "Why the fuck did you take that shot?" Eli yelled. His voice echoed through the ravine. The volume surprised him.

"We're legal 'til a half-hour after sunset," his dad said.

"We're on someone else's property," Eli said. His dad didn't reply. Eli was about to start walking again but he thought he heard a faint noise. The wheeze of a small engine?

His dad kept going.

"Dad," Eli said. "Do you hear that? I think there're four wheelers up there. We need to climb out of here."

"They can come down here if they wanna talk," his dad said. "I'm tracking a deer."

"It's dark out," he said. "You're not tracking shit. And you just shot at a fucking deer on their property."

"That was *your* deer."

"You don't know that."

"They don't either," his dad said.

"You can explain that to whoever the hell is up there."

His dad marched up the hill, his shotgun flung over his shoulder, and he emerged from the woods and into a field where three men wearing camo jackets sat on four-wheelers. The men were focused on his father, not looking in his direction. Eli crouched behind a tree and took off his blaze orange hat. One of the men, fully bearded, got off his four-wheeler and started pointing at Eli's dad. His dad knew how to handle these situations. He'd been in the military: he could take orders; he could give orders.

His dad took off his hat and wiped his brow, never once looking over in Eli's direction. He could hear his dad say "my son" and "wounded deer" and "I'm really sorry." Pretty soon, after they'd talked for a bit more, he heard the men laughing.

The snow was coming, a bit faster now. It was dark but the snow made it light enough to see.

His dad had rested his gun against an elm. He was standing tall, talking with his hands. When Eli sensed the situation was under control, he came out from behind the tree. But instead of walking over to his dad's defense, he stood there for another minute, trying to figure out what he wanted to say.

A
REAL
FUTURE

On this particular day, Gerald planned to pick up his new Firefighter license plates. He stood at the picture window, sipping his coffee in silence. Birds flittered in the backyard— the manic flapping of wings, prancing around snow-matted prairie grasses and bird feeders, and pecking at dead tree limbs. He took note of the sparrows, redwing black birds, blue jays, cardinals, and woodpeckers that swooped through the prairie and around the oak trees at the edge of the field. Gerald started most mornings this way, drinking coffee and watching the birds, contemplating what was next.

After a successful stint at Camcar Manufacturing, and after reluctantly accepting a retirement buyout package six months prior to this, Gerald found himself with time on his hands. As such, he started things he hadn't found time to do previously. He made coffee every morning; concocted plans to visit extended family; took on long neglected home improvement projects; and, finally, joined the volunteer firefighters' crew, something he did on a whim. Still, he usually woke early and agitated; a scratching need to be at work or out of the house; to be doing something. Which is why, on this day, he felt a sense of purpose.

As he warmed his hands on the ceramic mug, Denise, his wife, approached him, kissed him on the cheek. "Are you going to put the plates on the Buick or the Cadillac?"

Gerald chuckled.

"It's nice to see you smile," she said.

"I'm glad you still have your sense of humor," Gerald said.

The Caddy was now semi-retired as well, sleeping under

a tarp in the garage. It only came out in late spring, after all the sand and salt had been cleared from the roads, and put back in storage late fall. It had been a gift from his late father, a mechanic, who'd won the vehicle in a game of dice against Bill Jackson, their neighbor. At the time, mid-'70s, the Caddy wasn't in running condition. Gerald's father had restored it, and gave it to him as a gift when Gerald moved from Waterloo to Decorah at the age of twenty-two.

"I'll see you later tonight?" she said.

"After our meeting, I might go out with the guys," he said.

He kissed her once more on the cheek before she left for school.

Gerald continued to sip his coffee. He thought of the days when he was nineteen, cruising up and down the Waterloo strip in the Caddy, listening to his father's 8-tracks: Otis Redding, Stevie Wonder, Roberta Flack. His friend Walter sitting passenger-side and *Tell the Truth* turned way up. The boys often cruised around looking for Ruby and Deloris, but mostly they just drove and listened to music.

Gerald refocused on his plans for the day. He imagined the shiny new plates on his Buick—the red lettering on white background and the attention he might receive as the plates were a sign of his membership with this group. The volunteer firefighters. As he thought of this, a flock of juncos landed under his birdfeeder and instantly started pecking seeds out of the snow and grass. It was a good sign, as the junco was his favorite seasonal bird. They were playful birds that rarely landed in the feeders, but spent most of their time on the ground, foraging on whatever the other birds pushed out. They were mostly gray, but with a white patch on their underbelly, and stunning, almost mesmerizing, dark eyes.

● ● ●

His Buick warmed up in the driveway as he brushed off snow,

and scraped ice from the windshield. It was March in the Midwest, but winter was having a tough time leaving or giving any indication thereof. Gerald went inside for a Phillips screwdriver. He knew there were better tools for taking off license plates, but this particular Phillips had a wide head, and should work well enough.

●　　●　　●

Gerald parallel parked out front of the courthouse. He took the stairs one at a time, his hand on the railing. Even in town, there were still patches of snow and bits of ice on the concrete. No need to rush.

The courthouse was a stately, powerful structure, and Gerald always felt a sense of grandiosity while walking into the building. He opened the old wooden doors and was met with a blast of heat. Signs hung from the ceiling, denoting hallways and offices. In the City Clerk's office, he told the receptionist his situation.

"We'll need to exchange the plates for your old ones," said the woman behind the counter. She was younger than Gerald, but there was something about her that seemed haggard, old. He imagined she was a working mother of at least two kids.

"So you want me to bring in the ones on my car?"

"Right," the woman said. She was leaning on the counter holding the plates, which were wrapped in clear plastic, red lettering on a shiny white background. "Iowa" was written above and "Fire Fighter" below the actual license number, and a Firefighter decal shone on the left. Gerald felt an extraordinary sense of pride. He reached out, touched the plates. The woman secured her hold.

"Don't worry," he said. "I'm just checking them out." Their eyes met for just a moment, and he could sense her letting down whatever guard she'd put up. Making eye contact was something he wasn't able to do when he first moved here. Even now, he could count on two hands the number of black people in Winneshiek County.

Gerald pulled the Phillips out of his winter jacket, held it proudly, waving it in the air, patting the palm of his hand with the tip of the screwdriver. He smiled at her, a big toothy smile.

"Just give me a couple minutes," he said to the woman behind the counter. "I'll be right back with the plates."

On the way back to his vehicle, Gerald hugged himself against the cold. It was that long transitional time from winter to spring. Some years were quicker than others, but not this year. This year it was thaw, freeze, thaw, freeze, snow, thaw, snow, and on it went.

He clutched the handrail, shuffling along in his winter boots, scarf tied tight. The wind always whipped around this time of year and he could feel it seep into his pants and legs. Before taking the rest of the steps to the street, he paused, looked up at the pure blue sky, fresh and open. He breathed in the Iowa air. He felt something close to hope. He patted his pocket to make sure the screwdriver was still there.

Other cars were parked close to his front and back bumpers. He took notice for a moment trying to think of how he was going to do this. He didn't want to get down on his hands and knees in public, to be seen squatting next to a car. Pride, perhaps. He wondered if working on the ground was something fifty-eight-year-old men did in public. He felt around on his right side, the clip on his belt that held the firefighter walkie-talkie. There were occasional reports, often nothing serious. But if a series of three beeps came through, that was an emergency situation. There were rarely any, but there were often general call-in reports: a gas leak, a cat in a tree, a deer stuck in a sink hole, an unruly bonfire. Not often were they called for an all-house, burn-to-the-ground fire.

"Gerry!" someone shouted. A Ford F-250 rolled up to

where Gerald stood next to his Buick. "What's up, man?"

"Oh, hey, Lance," Gerald said. "Finally getting my plates." He pointed back toward the courthouse. The wind picked up and Gerald could feel himself being pushed by the westerly breeze.

"Good for you," Lance said. "See you at the meeting?"

"Of course," Gerald said.

Before Lance sped off, he pointed at Gerald. "Good to see you, man!"

Gerald never knew how to respond to this kind of enthusiasm, so he put a hand up to wave goodbye, and watched Lance's truck pull away. A bumper sticker read: *Spay & Neuter Liberals.*

Gerald did attend the Wednesday meetings and trainings. Some of the volunteer crew called it "church night" and others called it "Busch Light Night" or "BLN" because of what they did after their training. Gerald rarely made it out to the tavern, but he was often invited, often with a variety of backslaps, and generous voices encouraging him to come out and get rowdy with the guys. When he didn't go, he'd say to them: "Who the hell'd be available if something actually happened? I mean, guys, we need at least a half-sober driver."

This reply usually got a few knowing nods and chuckles. But when Gerald did go with the guys, he felt more like an observer than a participant, watching them guzzle their beers, reach for popcorn, and order more and more rounds until the middle of their table was a sea of brown bottles. Gerald ate from his own bowl of popcorn, having pulled up a seat that sat just far enough from the actual tables. He listened to the men talk about their upcoming softball leagues, their families, their jobs, their hobbies, their complaints about life. Gerald would finish his two beers and wave as he walked toward the door. But as he was about to leave he'd hear: "Already, Gerry? C'mon, stay for one more."

He'd nod politely, put his hand up one more time, and

slip out. He didn't understand their insistence. But he decided after Lance pulled away that he would join them at the tavern tonight.

Squatting next to his vehicle, Gerald pulled the Phillips from his coat pocket and got down on his knees. He lined the screwdriver up with the bottom right screw and began to turn, but his efforts were in vain. He tried again, but with no luck. Then he tried again, and again, and again. He realized he'd been holding his breath, so he stood up, exhaled, and then inhaled the cold air. A woman walked by pushing a stroller. The infant was bundled completely, so that all you could see were eyes, nose, and mouth. Gerald waved, smiled, and said, "Hello," and the woman did the same. He watched her walk away, and then he started laughing. At first it was light laughter, and then he found himself in a fit. He tried to keep himself contained, but the image of Lance's bumper sticker, *Spay & Neuter Liberals*, was so over-the-top, and so far from his own political beliefs, as to be at first amusing, and now hilarious. Gerald's shoulders shook up and down. His laugh was a light wheeze. He folded his arms, said it out loud a few times, "Spay and Neuter Liberals." Then, when he couldn't control his laugh anymore, he put a hand over his mouth and shook his head, chuckling into his hand.

He got on the ground and tried again: the bottom left screw, the right one, the top left, then top right, all of which were somehow rusted and sealed tight. So tight in fact that Gerald hadn't made one move. He clutched his wrist, which was sore now from the strain. Christ almighty, he thought, still on his knees in the crunchy, dirt-snow that lined the edges of the street. He chuckled once more, a tremor. He looked up at the court house.

●   ●   ●

Inside the City Clerk's office Gerald took off his stocking cap, undid his maroon scarf so that it dangled down his chest. He felt warm. "I have proper tools at my house," he told the woman at the counter. "And look," Gerald said, "I live a ways out, five miles. All a person needs is a hairdryer to warm them screws and the right bit driver."

"But unfortunately I can't give these to you, sir, until I have the ones on your car," the woman said. She leaned on the counter in the same way she had before. The counter was tall, marble, solid, a relic from the past.

"I'd like those plates to take with me," Gerald said. "I'll change them out and next time I come to town, I'll drop off my old ones."

"I believe that you would, sir, but still," she said. "It's a strict policy."

A flash of heat swelled up through Gerald's stomach and into his limbs. He unzipped his jacket, took off his gloves and set them on the counter next to his stocking cap.

"Ma'am, look," Gerald said. "I'll send them in with my wife first thing tomorrow morning. She works over at the school. You know, Denise Yates?"

"I do know, Denise, Mr. Yates, yes, I do," she said. "But I can't give these out until I have the ones they're replacing." The woman clutched the plates. Gerald set his hand on the light colored marble. He'd used this tactic before, mostly when they were first married, drawing on his wife's name, a well-respected teacher in the community, to exact some legitimacy for himself.

"I'd like to talk to your supervisor," Gerald said.

"I'm sorry, these are the policies, and talking to anyone above or below me will not change the outcome."

"Good-god, they're plates for chrissake." Gerald paused, aware of the others watching. "Would you please just get someone else? That's all I'm asking. I'm not asking for the plates anymore. I'm asking to speak with someone else."

"About what?"

Gerald pulled his hat and gloves back on. "Look, I have no interest in a confrontation, here."

"Then you should probably leave, sir," said another worker behind his cubicle. He stood up. He was a rather large fella with glasses and a polo shirt and jeans. "You heard, Linda. Those plates will be here for you tomorrow." Gerald noticed the name plate next to her desk.

"Linda, are you going to find a supervisor for me to talk to?" Gerald said, his voice calm.

The new guy, in his short-sleeved polo, walked around his cubicle and stood next to Linda.

"Mr. Yates, these are your plates, and they will be your plates tomorrow. We just need your old ones. This is not about trust or anything else—"

"So now you don't trust me?" Gerald said.

"I'm trying to tell you we do trust you," Linda said. She looked at her colleague.

"I'll be back."

● ● ●

Inside his vehicle, Gerald dialed his mechanic, a guy he'd known for years. "The damn things are just stuck," Gerald said.

"Sometimes they just mold together solid and there ain't nothing nobody can do," the mechanic said. "Bring it on down and I'll just slap your new ones over the old. That's what we usually do with those stubborn plates."

"That ain't gonna work," Gerald said. "I need to exchange the old ones to get the new."

"I've never heard of that," the mechanic said.

"For Firefighter plates," Gerald said. "Exchange needed for those."

"No shit?" the mechanic said. "That's great news. How long you been a firefighter?"

That was the general response from most people when he told them—half excitement, half disbelief that someone Gerald's age would be a new member of the volunteer squad.

"I'm in my probationary year," Gerald said. "After that they vote on my admittance, or whatever." What Gerald didn't say is that after his probationary period he'd more than likely have one or, at most, two years left of eligible service given the approximate retirement age for their county branch was sixty. During the probationary period he wouldn't be able to drive the truck, or even be on the first one out to a fire-call. And if he were fully active the next year, his age would probably prevent the same thing. Still, Gerald didn't think or worry about that. Not yet, anyway.

"Well, tell you what," the mechanic said. "Bring it by and I'll take a look."

●   ●   ●

The process to become a volunteer firefighter was time-consuming. Three nights a week for six months, Gerald and several other guys from neighboring counties would take the three-hour-long classes. It was serious, sure, but there was also a lot of laughing and sarcastic comments that Gerald didn't really find funny: white people humor, his father used to say. Also, he wasn't sure what to make of all the faux-friendly back-slaps and outrageous comments about sexual performance or small jabs at one's riding lawn mower—those things just weren't humorous to Gerald. Regardless, he enjoyed the process of becoming a volunteer firefighter; he felt proud of the time invested, and satisfied with the idea that he could learn something new. And it had given him something to focus his restless energy. He often wondered what his own father might think of him working as a firefighter, investing in the community. He imagined a deep sense of pride. His father, after all, was the one who told him, on the evening before he left Waterloo: "Never in a million years, young Negro, come back to this place. This is a hard place, and you have a future—*a real future*—somewhere else."

●　●　●

On his way to Bob's auto-shop, Gerald started to question his motivation for the plates. All this hassle for something new and shiny to show-off. When he was in those evening training sessions, many of the teachers—experienced firefighters—had those plates. They were instantly recognizable in the parking lot, stuck out in an attractive way, and Gerald, upon seeing them for the first time, made that his goal. He wanted to be recognized; he wanted to see the look of recognition on people's faces when they realized he was in fact part of the revered volunteer crew. But now, with all the hang ups, he thought himself silly over the episode.

Still, he drove into Bob's Shop.

"This is a bear," Bob said, using all the leverage he could muster. "Rusted shut, man." Bob applied spray-on lubricant, tried again. He used a blow-dryer to heat things up, tried again. No luck.

"What can we do?"

"Well, let's see if this young buck can help." Bob hollered at a young man half Gerald's age. Bob sprayed on more WD-40, and then the young man took a heavy set of pliers and muscled the screws loose. Once they started turning, they came off without issue. The young man held all eight screws in his hand, showing Gerald and Bob the rust around the grooves.

Gerald thanked both men, offered to pay, but they wouldn't accept the money. "Buy us a beer sometime," Bob said, referring to the youngster and himself.

"Will do," Gerald said. "I'd like that."

●　●　●

Gerald drove to the courthouse without plates on either end of his vehicle, but it was a short drive, a mile at most. Hell, everything was a mile at most around town. Sometimes Gerald wondered why he lived so far out when he could be walking everywhere. Sometimes he'd forgotten why he and Denise moved away from town in the first place, and as he crossed the bridge over the Upper Iowa River, Gerald thought that maybe this wasn't a place, a town, a home, he knew very well. Over the last few weeks and months, now having more time to spend in city limits, he felt as if he were getting reacquainted with a town that he'd ignored. Or that had ignored him. Or maybe, living out in the country, he was just disconnected. He wasn't sure.

●　●　●

Back in the '80s, when they'd first met, he and Denise were the only mixed couple in town. And for every person who accepted their relationship—those friendly people who would wave and say "hello"—there were just as many, or more, who didn't. People who'd ask Denise: *What's it like? Being with a black man? Do you trust him? Is he violent? Has he ever hit you? Does he do drugs? Does he sell drugs, I mean that fancy car?*

At first Denise entertained some of these questions, tried to fend them off with indignant rebuttals, but soon she confided to Gerald that she felt looked down upon by those who questioned her, even people she considered close friends. And those questions were tame in comparison to the harassments that would leave her badly shaken. The first time someone yelled "nigger-lover" from their truck, she spent the first hour of the school day in the principal's office crying, trying to find composure, before conducting class.

After the second such verbal assault the couple started to build a wall around themselves, hardly leaving their home, except for work and weekend drives in the Caddy. And eventually, after they'd been married a few years, they built a house on the outskirts of town. By then, Gerald had been promoted several times and was a floor manager, a foreman, at the manufacturing company. He was well-liked and respected by his team as well as higher-level management. Denise had put in several successful years teaching, earning many note-worthy county and state awards. The couples' combined salaries and frugal lifestyle allowed them to purchase ten acres of land and build a modestly-sized home. It wasn't the home Gerald had imagined, living this far from town, but he knew that establishing roots, somewhere, anywhere, as his father had told him, was important. Still, he never felt completely settled.

● ● ●

Now, driving across the bridge toward the courthouse, he turned on the oldies station. He found it hopeful that *Higher Ground* was playing. He tapped the wheel with his thumbs. He looked down at the water. The river's edges were still icy, and geese stood in the current, facing upstream, fishing and foraging for food. The town had seen an increase in the number of Canadian geese, and this year, the majority of the flock never went further south because of the open water here. He was in awe of the geese, like little statues standing in the frigid cold current. While others sat on top of the ice, bundled together and sitting so still that one might mistake them for decoys.

As Gerald came to the other side of the bridge, slow rolling at less than twenty-five miles per hour, still drumming on the steering wheel, he didn't notice the red light. It was a street light that hardly turned at all, and he often wondered, while passing it, if he'd ever run it.

As he coasted through the T-intersection, another vehicle had turned onto the street, and sped out in front of him. Gerald slammed on his brakes, but still nudged the car's bumper. He knew immediately it was just a light tap. Still, they pulled into the parking lot of an ice cream parlor closed until the weather got warmer.

"Ma'am," Gerald said, getting out of his car. "I am truly sorry."

She hunched over, surveying the stainless bumper. A medium sized mutt stood next to her on leash. "Looks like nothing." She laughed with relief.

"Exactly," Gerald said. "Nothing at all." He put a hand on the bumper and rubbed it.

"Well," she said. "Better notify police, just to be sure."

"I'm not sure if that's necessary," Gerald said. "I've gotten into these kinds of things before. I mean, people tapping my bumper in parking lots and whatnot, and no harm, no foul, you know what I mean?"

"I do," she said. "But my husband would be upset if I didn't at least report it, just to be safe."

"Let me assure you ma'am," Gerald said. "Well, actually, here, take my number. I'll write it down. You call me if there seems an issue after your husband looks at it."

"He's out of town." The woman pulled a phone from her purse.

"I really don't think this is necessary," Gerald said. He was trying to stay calm, knowing that any police officer would see that nothing was the matter, and, at the very most, he might get a ticket for running a red light. "Do what you need to do," he said to her. He put his hands on his hips and watched people drive by. It was mid-day and the traffic was picking up. Gerald looked away from the woman as she fumbled with her phone. The church steeple that sat high on the hill a few blocks away appeared brighter against the clear sky.

"Yes," the woman said into the phone. "I'm just calling to report a fender-bender, nothing serious."

Gerald was relieved at the woman's tone. He stuck his hands in his pockets, since his gloves were in his car. He swayed back and forth to an unfamiliar tune playing in his head that he'd heard on the radio on the way to town. The mutt looked at him, stuck its nose into his knee. Gerald tried to swipe the dog's nose away, gently.

"No, no one's hurt," she said into the phone. "Nope, no damage." She pulled the phone away, "Sadie," the woman said, "leave him alone."

Gerald smiled.

The woman stayed on the phone for a few minutes, gave her contact information, then clicked her phone shut.

"I guess we're good to go," she said to Gerald.

"That's great," Gerald said. "Do you still want my number?"

"Nah," she said. "Unless you're talking about something else." She winked at Gerald.

"Oh," Gerald said.

"I'm just messing with you," she said.

"Right, right," Gerald said.

"Well I hope this weather turns warmer sooner than later," the woman said. The dog stuck its nose in Gerald's crotch. "Sadie!" She pulled on the leash. "Sorry about that," she said to Gerald.

"That's okay," he said, smiling.

"The weather report shows more sunshine and warmer weather later this week."

"You know," Gerald said. "I figure it'll happen when it happens, ain't much we can do—talking or otherwise—that'll change that."

"I hear they got snow up north in the Twin Cities."

"Well, good thing we don't live there." Gerald looked

away. The woman's dog sniffed around Gerald's feet.

"And freezing rain in the Dakotas."

"Such is spring," he said.

"Blizzards in New England," she said.

"The weather's gonna do what it does." Gerald's face went hard, then immediately softened. After that comment, he noticed her physically shift away from him. He forced out a laugh to offset the noticeable change in her demeanor. "Tell me," he said, smiling at her. "What kind of dog is this?"

In front of the courthouse, finally, Gerald bent down and slipped the shiny plates out of their plastic sleeve and screwed both into their rightful places. He walked around, a full circle, the bright white and red of the plate gleaming against his navy blue vehicle which was covered in country dust. Around the courthouse several birds, the same ones he usually saw around his house, sputtered and whirled around bare branches. Juncos, sparrows, a few blue jays. He considered their indifference to the wind and cold, and for a split second, Gerald wished that he felt happier, somehow more elated about his plates. He wished his father could see them, and he wished, also, at that moment, that his father would've visited him, at least once, after moving away. All of their get-togethers happened in Waterloo, and only at Gerald's prompting. But his father, he imagined, would've liked this town—the buildings, the cleanliness, and (most of) the people. Many of whom were honest, hard-working, blue collar folks, like his father.

Gerald had some time before his meeting, so he decided to get into his car and cruise around, showing off his new plates.

For a moment, he wished it were summer, and he wished he was in his Caddy with Denise. But being in the Buick, with his new plates, was just fine. He drove slowly through downtown, keeping an eye on the people's faces. Would anyone take notice?

As he drove, there were recognizable faces everywhere—acquaintances and shop owners walking and driving through downtown—but no one seemed to pay any mind to his new plates. Or to Gerald for that matter, and maybe, he thought, this was because like most things that become part of your everyday, you don't notice them. You don't pay mind to what's always there. You take for granted that it'll be here today, tomorrow, and thereafter. And maybe this was because *he* had become part of the everyday, part of the community, even if on the periphery. He thought, then, that maybe this wasn't such a bad thing. But for some reason, even thirty-six years later, Gerald didn't want to let go of the idea that his *real* home, his roots, were elsewhere, with *his* people. But if creating a new home was something he always wanted—in whatever shape or form it might be—well, maybe this was it.

Gerald got to the end of town, and, with nowhere else to go, he went around the block and turned back onto the main drag. Gerald turned the radio back on. He kept driving.

EAST OF ELY

We stopped caring about how we actually felt toward one another a long time ago because our feelings fluctuated like spring temperatures in the Midwest. Instead, we devoted ourselves to each other in the old-fashioned way of loyalty and partnership. It wasn't a sexy, Hollywood endeavor—our marriage—but that was all about to change.

I should tell you now that I won't get into the specifics of our actual lives. That is, our names, jobs, etc., but as we get to the part I really want to tell you about, I think—I hope— you'll understand why.

What I will tell you, though, is that we married under what you might call societal pressures. She was pregnant before we were married, and really, there's not much else to say about it. We went on about our lives and everything was more or less fine until a month before our twenty-fifth wedding anniversary, when I lost my job and she decided we needed something different.

"We need an adventure," she said to me while gardening in the backyard. She was planting something.

"What do you have in mind?"

"I have ideas," she said, "but I don't think you have the stomach for them."

"Try me." I looked up from the push mower I was tinkering with, changing a spark plug.

"Why have I always felt attracted to banks?" she said.

"Oh, Lord," I said.

Here's the other thing you need to know about my wife: she was, and is, a kleptomaniac. We can't go into a gas station without her walking out with some ornament or pin, something small enough to conceal in her palm.

"I've got it staked out," she said.

"Risk factor?"

"I wouldn't have brought it up if there was much of any."

"I was thinking a nice dinner, you know? Maybe a movie. Dinner and a movie? You ever heard of that?"

"You were always so predictable, darling."

We were both forty-five years old, empty-nesters. My wife was slender in an overworked sort of way, and I was just developing what my kids called a beer-belly, despite not drinking much anymore.

"What are you planting?" I was trying to change the subject.

"Transplanting," she said. "Raspberries. Damn things are like weeds and I don't want them next to the garage anymore." The bandana around her forehead was wet. The sun was out and the sky was a perfect blue. "We should start taking our country drives again, too," she said. "I always liked those sleepy afternoons on the open road."

"All of a sudden we need to spend more time together?"

"Seems like a nice thing to do, that's all," she said. "Seems like a thing any married couple might do."

What wasn't a thing any married couple might do was rob a bank. But that's exactly what we did. On June 12th, the day of our twenty-fifth anniversary, we walked into the Ely Credit Union wearing masks, holding canvas bags, and clutching plastic pistols that we purchased at the Dollar Tree, and we used them to paralyze the bank staff while a teller—previously designated by my wife—unlocked the tills of money.

It was a beautiful spring day, lush trees and soft grasses that made you want to sing songs from your childhood.

Ely was a village just outside of Cedar Rapids, surrounded by large swaths of timber. The actual village was just a few houses and as many abandoned buildings, but there was this one, lone bank in the middle of nowhere on some county road that connected to nothing, just a few miles outside of Ely. Apparently, my wife had staked out the place for two months prior, hiding behind trees across the street, observing which days and times were busiest. She even knew which teller she wanted to mark. She said she chose the woman because of her predictable nature: parked in the same spot, chewed gum, wore her hair and carried her purse the same way, and always—always—held an unopened bottle of Diet Coke while walking into the bank.

The predictability, my wife argued, was a sign of some due diligence on her part to create a life of least resistance— that if she was put to a task, like helping us unlock money tills, she'd surely not fight or talk back, but instead do what she was told to do, and with efficiency. She was blond, and reasonably attractive, but only by virtue of her effort. Makeup, nails, hair fashion. My wife pegged her for a Target shopper, fake-baker, college Business major who slept around with endless frat boys in the hopes that one would eventually be fond enough to take her as a spouse. My wife was unusually perceptive about these things, and once, while we were on the last stakeout before our heist (the only one I attended), I spotted the woman walking into the bank and I knew right away she was the mark. I thought: my wife is exactly right.

My wife brandished her toy pistol, requested that all bank employees move to one corner of the room. "Nobody panic," she said. "We're not gonna hurt you. Now move." She was speaking in this falsetto British accent that she failed to warn me about. I thought it a deft move and chimed in with my own.

"Move quickly," I said, but it sounded more Australian than British.

"You," my wife said, sticking the pistol in the back of the mark, "come with me." The mark squealed a little, but obeyed, just as my wife had figured. Up close, I realized the woman wasn't in fact good-looking at all. She was all show. Not an ounce of natural beauty. Just fake nails, fake tan, and poorly highlighted hair, and it occurred to me at that very moment how deeply grateful I was that my wife—my partner—didn't feel a need for such show.

The other bank employees cowered toward the ground, moving like snails. "Quickly," I said again, trying to adjust my accent to match my wife's.

I walked over to where the other employees were commanded to wait and kept an eye on the three who squatted down, huddled against the corner, facing the wall. No one whispered a word, cried, or whimpered, and while my adrenaline surged, I became so hyper-focused that every movement of every person, even just the slightest slide of a finger or a leaning one way or the other, etched itself permanently into my memory. I can recall, even today, with great accuracy, every second we were actually inside the bank: the nervous twitch under an eye; the hostages shifting weight from one knee to the other; the bead of sweat that ran down one's cheek; the smell of flowery hand soap; the dark stain on the carpet next to one of the chairs (probably coffee); the unused look of the faux-leather couch; the way the teller's ponytail curled at the end, swaying slightly with every nervous movement.

The one male hostage was wearing gray slacks and a navy blue shirt, and I remember thinking that he looked quiet dapper, dressed up in a way to make himself appear more competent than he actually was. Maybe not so different from our mark in this way. The other two employees—women of about forty—were dressed like our mark, except both were brunettes, and both wore nondescript sets of earrings, and some low-heeled shoes. The practicality of which didn't go unnoticed, and I was glad that my wife had picked who she picked, because the others—more practical, more prepared women—might've out-flanked us, might've made a move for which we weren't ready. And I think that's the thing about life. Even at our most spontaneous we're still doing things within the realm of what we're fit for, and in this case our mark's always been fit for compliance, the path of least resistance. My wife, on the other hand, has always been fit for thievery. Like Michael Jordan's jump shot, or Magic Johnson's ability to dish out the ball, my wife was a natural born thief, and watching her work was a thing of beauty: the way she so elegantly glided around, giving orders. This was her most ambitious take yet, and I knew, after we got out of there, it wouldn't be our last. And it wasn't.

"Scoot your ass over to the corner with the others," my wife said. She shooed the mark away. The tills were open and she was filling bags. I signaled our mark with a motion of my toy gun to hustle. Her high heels tapped the wood floors. My wife stuffed the canvas bags full of bills. I knew, for her, it didn't matter if they were ones or one-hundreds; this take was about so much more than the money.

As our mark walked past me, she looked back at my wife, turned toward me, and tripped over the threshold between the wood floor and carpet. She fell head-first into a desk. The collision made a loud, unsettling smack. And instantly there was blood everywhere—on her face, the floor.

"What the hell happened?" my wife said, still in her best British accent.

I knelt down to the woman who was crying and clutching her head. "Ouch," I said. "That doesn't look good."

"Let me help," one of the women next to the wall said.

"Nobody moves," my wife said. She was back to her normal voice. A slight Midwestern drawl.

The blood pooled quickly. I knew this from my days in basketball. A guy gets elbowed in the face, the head, and it bleeds. I mean, bleeds. And that's what our mark was doing.

"She'll be fine," I said to no one in particular. "Just a lot of blood."

The woman squirmed and made noises on the ground, tiny whimpers, and I felt an uncommon urge to reassure her that she would in fact be okay. I reached out and touched the woman's leg. She flinched, flung her right arm at me as if she were trying to simultaneously shoo me away *and* backhand me. As she did this, she accidentally slapped my right hand, the one holding the pistol, and dislodged the plastic gun from my grip, sending it flying across the lobby. It sailed—the pistol—in an arch, toppling sideways over itself, until finally it hit the counter that my wife stood behind. As it connected with the counter a less-than-sufficient thud filled the room, and when that happened, all four of the hostages looked at me, then my wife, then back at me, and there was for a moment this palpable breech in conduct. All of a sudden, I was simply a guy in a bank with no weapon, no gun, therefore no power, and the looks on the hostages' faces told a hundred different stories all at once. I glanced at my wife and the story I told her, without speaking of course, was to get the fuck out of there as soon as possible. Which we started to do.

But that didn't stop the guy dressed in gray slacks, blue shirt and tie, from confronting me. He didn't address the fake gun issue because there was no need. We all knew. Instead, he emerged slowly while the other employees stayed on the floor, and stepped toward the bleeding woman, checked on her, then leveled his gaze at me. I can't tell you now that I felt completely in control. I didn't. But I wasn't altogether scared either. I was mostly calm, and as he approached me, with my wife still behind the counter, now moving toward the door, I remembered my pocket knife and pulled it out: four-inch blade, stainless, spring-loaded, so it flipped open with ease.

"You come near us," I said, "and I'll slice your throat." The guy stopped. My hand shook. My heartbeat quickened.

This, of course, wasn't part of the plan. We were improvising. We were establishing a new path. When I said this, my wife stopped, stood next to me, clutching three canvas bags, each of which ballooned out to the size of a soccer ball.

Then, instead of walking straight out the door, she turned toward the bank employees. "Nobody moves for five minutes," she said.

"Yeah, right," the guy said. "Second you morons walk out, cops are on your ass—you'll never get away with this, you and your fake guns."

She leveled her toy pistol on the guy's forehead with an unwavering confidence. The action made everyone in the room momentarily wonder if hers was fake or real. You could see a definite moment of hesitation reorient his face.

"Like I said," my wife said. "Stay put for five minutes, or I will torch each of your houses." Then, in yet another surprising move, she started reciting the names and addresses of each of the employees. Actually, she only got through the names of the other two women. Then she said to those women, "I'll come to your homes and fuck your husbands, kill your children, and burn everything to ash if you even so much as think of moving before five minutes are up."

It was her best British accent yet.

We hustled out the glass door. A wave of fresh, spring air. "Nice speech," I said, trying for my best Brit, but it sounded more Irish this time. We hopped into our Taurus—which we no longer own—and drove off.

My wife drove, and I rode shotgun with the money at my feet. For a while we didn't talk, just enjoyed the drive, the open road. The windows were down and her gray-brown hair flew all around her, some of it wrapping around her face. I could tell by her silent look of satisfaction that she was as pleased with this day as any other we'd shared.

We maneuvered onto some gravel roads, kicking up dust behind us, the sun high and strong, and the fresh air infusing everything around us with the promise of a beautiful summer.

"Where to?" I said, breaking our silence.

"East of Ely," she said. "To a land of lush forests and vast prairie—a place where no one will bother us." She leaned over, patted me on the knee. "Good work, darling."

We pulled into an abandoned farmstead, which was yet another surprise. It was an old turn-of-the-century Victorian that butted up against a wooded hillside in back, and a field of prairie grass out front, just as she'd said.

She got out, lifted a dilapidated garage door. She got back in, pulled the car inside. Then she led me into the empty house where she had already set up an air mattress, picnic basket, blanket, three bottles of wine (which I considered at that moment a bit excessive), and a handheld radio that she turned on to some jazz station that neither of us ever listened to before. She grabbed me then, brought me close, and we danced to some musician's sad saxophone.

We made love that night in a way that I can only describe as reckless and desperate—the way we sloppily kissed and clung to each other, the way we flopped around on that air mattress, and later, outside in the still spring night, on a bed of thick grass.

And later still, in the wee hours of the night, we lay in bed, sipping wine, whisper-talking about our dreams, how some of them had come true, while others had not. She also confessed to me all the times she'd thought about leaving, and I confessed to her the same. We talked about moments when we fought or ignored each other, stretches of our lives when we were simply enduring the daily grind, and she told me she used to occasionally pick fights with me just to feel something more than what she described as my "cruel indifference." I told her then that I'd never loved her more than I did at that exact moment. And that was true. And I made a promise to myself that night that I'd be a different person, for her and for me.

As the sun came up over the eastern tree line, filtering first-light through cloudy glass windows, I asked her what she wanted to do with the money. It was the first time either of us had thought to discuss it. Her head was propped on my shoulder as we lay naked under the quilt.

"I didn't have anything in mind," she said. "Nothing at all."

WE COULD'VE BEEN HAPPY HERE

I was back at Lyle's, farm-sitting. Even after the last episode out there he had the courage to invite me back. Circumstances were such. Plus, we'd been friends long enough and he thought to give me another chance. Lyle was always hoping the best for me.

How it came about: I'd been using for about a year, losing weight, eyes black from no sleep. My gums were just starting to recede, and the day before Lyle called, I'd started my basement apartment on fire brewing a batch in a plastic root beer bottle. My best buddy lost most of his hair and burnt part of his face in the explosion, and I knew then it was time. I dropped him off at the emergency room and left town after he'd been secured. That was about the time Lyle needed someone to farm-sit. Over the phone I told him *everything*. He listened for a while, and then there was a long pause like he was really thinking about things. He'd always been considerate in that way. Then he told me, "Lesson number one in kicking bad habits: get out of town, away from other users. Still," he said, "it won't be easy." Then he asked about my kids.

"Haven't seen them in a year," I said.

"Not good," he said.

•   •   •

First day on the farm, I puked twenty-five times, ran a fever, and drank Gatorade to keep hydrated. Lyle had stocked the fridge for me. I was partial to the purple kind. The second, third, and fourth days, I puked about fifteen times each day and stayed on a steady diet of Gatorade, barely getting chores done: feeding cows, moving electrical fences, etc. Finally, on day five, gaunt and still slightly feverish, I came through. My appetite returned. Every time I had a craving, I did pushups or sit-ups, or ran wind-sprints around the rolling pasture. The world looked painted in neon. Imagine coming out of a hangover: giddy and clearheaded, the world a bit brighter. I was like that for a few days, but with no one to talk to. When that clearheaded vision of the world wore off, sad, serious, introspective sobriety took over. And I was still shaky.

About the time I was feeling like I could just function, some guy came over looking for Lyle. He rumbled down the gravel driveway in his truck and rapped on the door. It was dark out. I stepped onto the porch.

"Where's Lyle?" he said.

I reached for the guy, hugged him, wrapped my arms around his chest. He was thick. I hadn't seen another human in days. This was Halloween weekend.

"What's this?" he said. "Do I know you?" He grabbed my arms and moved me away.

"We're strangers," I said. "I'm just glad to see someone. I can only talk to animals for so long."

He backed up out of the porch light. "Don't do that again," he said.

Then he introduced himself as Whitetail. He ran a hand down his white ponytail that hung long on his denim jacket. I did the same thing, and he said, "Mine used to be coal-black, just like yours." Then he said: "Where's Lyle?"

"Out of town," I said. "I'm farm-sitting."

Whitetail stepped inside the door. "Listen buddy," he said. "You've got a herd loose on Balsam Road, five miles south of here. I'd help you out but I'm pulling third tonight, driving to Omaha with a load of grain. New ethanol plant down there."

"I have no idea," I said.

"They're basically like distilleries," he said. "Making corn liquor, except they use it as fuel and—"

"—No, man," I said. "I had no idea about Lyle's herd five miles south of here. I'm only keeping track of a few animals around the barn and pastures near the house. I have no idea how to rally cattle."

Whitetail grabbed at his ponytail again, ran it through his thumb and forefinger. "Well," he said. "They're along the ditch and a small stretch of timber next to the road. Those ditches are pounded with herbicides, too." He smirked. "So much for his organic cattle."

Whitetail told me to get dressed, told me he'd take me up to see Earnest, Lyle's right-hand man. "He's a little ornery," Whitetail said. "But he's the only one Lyle trusts with those larger herds." And then he smirked again, like there was some joke he thought of but couldn't tell me.

Inside, I threw on layers of clothes and grabbed the buckeye that my friend, Katharine, had given to me. I'd been keeping it in my pocket, using it like a worry stone, rubbing my thumb over its smooth, rich brown surface. Then I scuttled through drawers and at the last second grabbed a Mini-Maglite and stuffed it into my vest pocket. Later that night, when I was trying to keep track of the cows moving around me, I'd find out the batteries were dying.

● ● ●

Earnest lived up the road, just off the blacktop, a mile past the church. Whitetail drove, parked, and then walked me up to the door. Earnest invited us in. He was wearing a Carhartt hoodie and jeans. His cheeks were red and splotchy.

Whitetail introduced me, and then told him the story about the cows. After that, Earnest walked to the couch and sat down. There were several people in his house—another man, woman, and four kids—and they all stayed seated, watching us. Whitetail patted me on the back. "Gotta roll," he said.

I offered my hand. "Appreciate it," I said. He shook my hand and I didn't want to let go. His hands were rough leather. I needed him to stay. These people—I felt like they had something against me. They gawked at me like I was some kind of carnival attraction.

Whitetail pulled his hand away and leaned in close. "Don't be a pussy," he said, whispering. Then, even quieter: "These fuckers are a little strange, but you should be fine. Earnest's got more cattle experience than anyone in the county."

"Great," I said. "Wonderful."

"All right," Whitetail said. Then he slipped out the door.

The people inside were all crammed into a living room with country-green walls. Hand-carved ducks and cows claimed the corners of the room. Balloons were tied to the kitchen chairs, and a cake sat on the table.

I heard Whitetail's truck fire up and pull out of the driveway. I watched his taillights fade. I stood on the welcome mat, just inside the door. No one invited me further. They all sat there, with a mutt lying on the floor, its tail slapping the carpet. The woman brushed cake crumbs off a toddler.

Then they started forking into their cake and sipping out of coffee mugs sporting phrases like, "Best Dad Ever." No one talked, not even the kids, and I just stood there in the foyer among the mess of work boots and kids' shoes, waiting. The clock on the kitchen wall showed a quarter to nine. A fluorescent light flickered. A Black & Decker coffee pot sat on the counter, and it occurred to me that the house smelled of hazelnut. Finally, the oldest kid, wearing a party hat, looked at me and said: "Would you like a piece of cake?" Her hair was cut into a sloppy bob, the kind my mom used to give my sisters.

I glanced at the adults. Earnest was forking into his last

bite of chocolate swirl cake. "Nah," I said. "I think I'm okay, but thanks."

"It's my birthday," she said. "I'm 9."

"That's great," I said. "Happy birthday."

"Why's your hair so long?" she said. Her voice was strong and mature. Matter-of-fact.

"Just letting it grow," I said.

"Are you an Indian?" she said. The adults in the living room, they all stopped mid-sip, mid-bite, and waited for an answer. By now, the other kids were balling up wrapping paper and throwing it in the air.

"Nope," I said. "Not an Indian, but I get that question all the time." I gave the girl a close-mouthed smile knowing everyone else was watching.

Then Earnest said: "You sure you're not Native or something?" The dog stood, stretched, and walked over to me. The tail was really working. I stuck out my hand and the dog licked it.

"Rowdy," Earnest said. "Leave him alone."

"I love dogs," I said.

"Rowdy," he said again.

"No, really, it's fine," I said.

"Rowdy, get your ass back here."

The dog trotted back and cowered next to the coffee table.

"So?" Earnest said. "Native?" I pulled off my stocking cap to confuse them a little more. I had my hair pulled back into a ponytail, as the girl had already observed. A couple years ago, after I wasted my girlfriend's paycheck on lottery pull tabs at a 24-hour gas station at two in the morning, and got picked up for drunk driving that same night, she took a bat to my motorcycle *and* my car. Then she left. After that, for whatever reason, I started growing my hair out. I haven't seen her since, and now my hair was halfway down my back. A week after the episode she left me a voicemail that said she was an all-state softball player back in the day and that knocking out my windows was better than any sex we'd ever had. I kept the message, and I listen to it every now and then. It was sad at first, but now I listen to it if I need a good laugh. If I have buddies over for poker, they beg me to play it.

"Nah, man," I said. "Not Native."

"You sure?" the other guy said. "Because I would've bet my meager life savings that you were Lakota. I had you as Lakota the second you walked into this house."

"Nope," I said, shaking my head.

"Well, what then?" the other guy said.

"Native to Iowa," I said.

The other guy slapped the table. "Well I'll be goddamned." He shook his head. He laughed. He was the only one.

Three toddlers with cake-covered chins had gathered on the floor in front of me. The birthday girl stood with them, studying my face. We made eye contact. Something about her was sad and beautiful, not unlike my own daughter, and I could see now, in her socially malnourished eyes, that her heart had already been broken, and if I could look into the future, I could tell you that it would happen a few more times. But she didn't need to know that. I kept it to myself. I thought I might be able to raise her—all these kids—along with my own. I kept that to myself too.

●　　●　　●

Earnest told me to meet him outside, next to his Oldsmobile. Anya, his daughter, the birthday girl, begged to come with.

"I don't give a shit," Earnest said. Then he shot a glance at Anya's mom.

"Whatever," the mom said. "I suppose it's her birthday."

Anya said, "Yes," to no one particular, then grabbed her coat and some glittery toy.

Before we got into the vehicle, I thanked Earnest for taking time to help but he made no motion that he heard me.

As we pulled onto the road, I said it again: "Thanks for coming. You really didn't have to do this."

"Cows have one stomach," he said. "Not four, like most people think." But he wasn't looking at me, he was looking out the window of the Olds. Then he added, "Their digestive compartments are made for grass, not grain, but it's tough to fatten them up on grass."

He kept on like that for a while. When I'd ask a question he'd throw out a random fact about cows, or he'd say whatever was on his mind.

He flipped through AM stations. We turned onto a gravel road and the loose rock pelted the underside. The headlights did nothing to help out. We drove for a few miles before the land started to drop—we were driving into some valley. The windows were down and the air grew cold and we could see our breath. "Gonna be a heavy frost tonight," he said.

"So, a good birthday party?" I said. Anya was singing quietly to herself.

"E. coli can't grow in the gut of a grass-fed cow," Earnest said.

"Didn't know that," I said.

We drove for a minute before he added, "It's the end of football season."

"I'm not much of a fan," I said. A guy on the radio announced the five-day forecast. "Who's your team?" I said.

"There was an article in the sports section," he said. "High school football: Decorah Vikings *scalp* Waukon Indians." He flipped to another station. "Politically correct hasn't made its way up here."

"Didn't read that article," I said.

"I clipped it to the fridge," he said.

We rumbled down the gravel. I rested my elbow against the window. A guy on the radio was talking about fishing in Northern Minnesota. Earnest turned the volume down. He looked at me. "So, you lying about being an Indian or Native American, or whatever the hell you call yourselves these days?"

I waited a few seconds, thinking of a decent response. "What do you think?" I said.

"I actually don't give a fuck," he said. "How about this, though: try celebrating your kid's birthday with your ex-wife and her husband, their two shithead kids, plus my two." The car was dark except for the numbers on the radio and dashboard. Earnest held the steering wheel with one hand. "I'm not here to help rally cows," he said. "Although I will do that. I'm here to get the hell out of the house. I felt like a rusty nail getting hammered into the knot of a two-by-twelve, getting all bent up, going nowhere."

"We might have a little in common," I said.

Anya went from singing to whistling.

"I started a list," Earnest said, "of creative ways to kill myself. Started the other day when I found out *I* was hosting the birthday. No offense, sweetheart," he said to his daughter. She kept whistling.

"Impressive," I said. "Now we're talking about something I'm interested in."

"There," he said, pointing out my window. We'd passed a cow. He put on the brakes. I touched my pocket, feeling for my buckeye. "You ready there, Anya?" he said.

"This is the best birthday party ever," she said. She unbuckled her seatbelt. She was the only one who'd buckled.

● ● ●

We stood at the edge of the gravel road, silent. I asked how the cows had gotten out of the pasture, and how many there were, and Earnest said, "Doesn't matter now, just matters that we get them rallied."

I looked over at Earnest but could barely see him. I thought he might be working out a plan. The moon had yet to show, if it would at all, so the stars were it. Darkness was thick. I felt my vest pocket, touching the flashlight. Earnest had no source of light.

He started walking up the gravel road, and then yelling into the night: "Ca-boss, Ca-boss!" It was uncomfortably loud, in the way drawing attention to yourself in a new place can be.

"What's ca-boss?" I said. He stopped calling.

"Short for come-bossy," he said. "A feeding call. You say it before you feed the cows grain, or whatever, and they get conditioned to it." He walked back to where I was standing. The cows stirred in the ditch and beyond, grazing, their feet rustling the grass. "But no need for these girls to run to a cow-call when they've got a buffet under their nose. Right, Chief?"

I didn't reply.

I thought we should make a plan, but I'd never tried to rally a group of rogue cattle, so I kept my mouth shut. Earnest started hollering again. I tried to make out tree limbs against the night sky. Anya stood next to me, quiet. She was swinging the toy she had brought, a magic wand, whipping it through the air. The cattle stayed in the wide ditch and the pasture munching on grass. We hadn't gotten a hard frost yet so the vegetation was still green. "Cattle love this shit," Earnest said. "This heavy grass is like Big Macs to them."

I didn't reply.

"Can't you hear them smacking away?" he said, as if my silence had contradicted him. "They're hungry bastards." His laughter echoed off the limestone bluff behind us. Anya brushed against my arm.

"You okay, kiddo?" I said. I set my hand on her shoulder. She stood still. Earnest walked off, still chuckling to himself.

In the hour I'd known him, I'd hardly seen a smile, let alone a laugh. I tried to picture him: head tipped to the sky, his mouth and eyes stretched in a villainous outbreak. I knew there'd be more laughing. Earnest was a dog smelling fear.

He knew I was out of my element. My knees had begun to ache and my arms grew antsy—a dull pain grew around my neck. It was cool out, but I was sweating like a beast in a sauna. These things happened when I needed a fix. But I was trying to keep it together, trying to keep from panicking. I didn't want to look like a fool in front of Anya, his little girl. The birthday girl.

Earnest stood a ways off, yelling: "Ca-boss, Ca-boss!" Then he said to me: "You ready to rally some cattle, Chief?"

I didn't answer, so Earnest kept calling. A wind picked up. Leaves rustled. I could sense large objects—the cows—moving around me and I had no idea where to start or what to do. I took a few deep breaths.

"Walk down the road about fifty yards," Earnest said. "Then hop in the ditch and push them up to me; just start walking my way, talking, slapping the ground with a stick. Zig-zag your way through the brush. All you need is one cow to start moving, then they'll all start. Got it, Chief?" He clapped his hands twice. "You should be a natural at this— just like herding buffalo."

"Your jokes aren't funny," I said.

"Lighten up," he said. "You want help, or not?"

"What if they run up to the road, or behind me?"

"We're making game-time decisions here," Earnest said. "I'm not worrying about anything until the last second."

"I don't know if I'm up for this," I said. "I've never—"

"—Like I said, just imagine buffalo—Tatonka, Tatonka."

"Where should I go?" Anya said.

"You go with Chief-No-Indian," Ernest said.

Anya wrapped her hand around mine. She was waving her magic wand. Even in the dark it somehow glittered. Her hand was cool and dry. She squeezed tight. With my other hand I held the buckeye, rubbing it with my thumb and forefinger. I felt relieved for the dark, so Earnest couldn't see.

"Where'd you get the wand?" I said. "A birthday present?" We'd walked a while, out of earshot.

Earnest hollered: "Ca-boss, Ca-boss!"

"It's from some doll I have," she said.

"All right," I said. "Well, I'm happy you brought it. I think we might need a magic wand." I was trying to sound encouraging, so she didn't feel dumb. I remembered that as a kid: feeling dumb around everyone. I didn't want Anya to feel the same way.

"How was your birthday party?"

"You were there," she said. "What'd you think?"

"Dazzling," I said. "But I could've used some of that coffee."

She squeezed my hand, then let go.

"I think you're trying your best," she said. I liked her confidence in me.

"Thank you," I said. "I've never done this before, but I am trying."

"I can tell," she said.

It's not often you pay attention to your breathing patterns, but that's exactly what I was doing. Deep, full breaths of crisp autumn air. With Anya to take care of, I felt light and focused, not shaky or nervous, and at that moment I was only concerned for her, not for herding cows. I felt, then, that we'd met so I could protect her. But I knew that wasn't true. Maybe I'd imagined that idea to give myself purpose. It was nothing but a thought. I would never see Anya again—this nine-year-old holding a magic wand, her sad, sweet face and oversized jacket. Who was I to say? She was braver than me.

"This is probably far enough," I said, stopping at a steep embankment. "Have your eyes adjusted?"

"Kinda," she said. "My mom makes me eat carrots. She says it'll help keep my eyes good."

"That's a myth," I said. "But you should probably eat them anyway." I looked down and could see her pale face and teeth. She looked like she was smiling. "Are you smiling?" I said.

She pointed directly away from us, toward the tree line. The moon was just starting to show—a big, faded-orange harvest moon. "A cow," she said. "It's right there." And sure enough, just a few feet from us, a Black Angus stood neck to the ground, chomping on grass. A northerly breeze stirred and I could see the silhouette of tree branches swaying.

"Get that wand ready," I said. "Start casting a spell on those cows."

Earnest was still shouting, but had decreased volume and frequency. I squeezed my buckeye.

"Here we come," I shouted up to him.

"About time," he said.

"Stay up on the road," I said to Anya. "And keep that wand going." She whipped it back and forth. The moon was coming, and it reflected off her wand and face. She waved vigorously. "Just like that," I said. "Perfect."

●　●　●

I moved through the ditch, trotting through the tall vegetation, trying to round up the cattle. Anya called down to me, "You ever gonna cut your hair?"

"Why do you ask?" I was zig-zagging, as Earnest had suggested. I stopped for a moment and took out my Mini Maglite. When I turned it on, its light stuttered. I slammed it into my palm. It worked just long enough for me to see a couple Angus up against the far tree line, and then it died. I ran over and kicked at the grass. They moved toward Earnest. I zig-zagged back to Anya. "I'm up here now," I said to her. "Keep up."

She skipped along the gravel road, her boots crunching over the rock. The cows seemed to be moving on their own now, and I'd stopped in the ditch. I put the buckeye back in my pocket. Anya stood at the edge of the road, still waving her wand. "I think you should keep your ponytail," she said. "Even if you catch grief from my dad."

"That right?"

"It makes you different," she said.

"I'll accept that as a compliment," I said.

"Do your kids like it?"

I paused a moment and replayed our previous conversations. The moon, along the horizon, rose quickly, lighting the area around us. "How'd you know I had kids?"

"Just a guess," she said. "All the adults I know have kids."

"Seems like a logical guess," I said. "My son likes it; my daughter doesn't seem to show interest one way or another."

"Are they at the farm with you?"

"No," I said.

"Too bad," she said. "When you see them, you can tell them about my wand."

"What the hell you two doing down there?" Earnest hollered. "Keep pushing." He was still a ways off. With the moonlight, I could see him marching up the ditch, trying to push the cattle toward the road. "I need you to bring these girls up farther, near me," Earnest said. He was probably right, but everything we were doing seemed pointless. The cows had made up their own minds.

"Come on," I said to Anya. I ran up on the cows, and that startled them into a good clip. They cantered through the ditch, near the tree line, which opened up into a field, and as I was running behind them, everything went well. I jogged back and forth for a while, pushing the cows, getting tired, my boots dragging, before I saw something peel off to my right. It was heading the opposite direction, fast. I stopped. The other cows, their hooves pounded the ground, their bodies brushed against the tall grass. Anya was keeping up, still on the gravel road.

"Why'd you stop?" she said.

I rested my hands on my hips. "Where do you learn to cast spells?" I said.

"I was born with it," she said. "But my powers are growing with each birthday. I'm feeling especially strong tonight."

"Like you could really make these cows move."

"Yes," she said. "They're subject to my great and mysterious power—ha, ha, ha." It was a low, diabolical cartoon chuckle.

"What other magic do you know?"

"All kinds," she said. I walked up the steep embankment and stood next to her. The wind shot down the road. My hands felt shaky again, but not because of the cool breeze. I knew I'd have to rally that last cow.

Earnest resumed yelling, and I could see the Angus up on the road. With the moon finally over the trees, and the cows running next to the white limestone bluff and over the gray gravel road, their bodies looked too big, oversized. I glanced over at Anya. My heart was already breaking, knowing this adventure would end and I'd be going home to an empty house, and Anya would be driving home with her dad. I moved my hand over my chest. The cows kept running, heading in the right direction.

"Did you see a cow move off that way?" I pointed directly away from the road.

Anya was silent. Her wand lay next to her leg, pointing to the ground.

"It's not your fault," I said. I brought my arm around her and pulled her close.

"My wand usually works," she said.

"Listen," I said. "I have a birthday present for you."

I stepped away from her and dug the buckeye out of my pocket. "Here," I said. I set it in her hand. She rubbed it with her thumb.

"My mom collects these and puts them in a basket on the kitchen table, for decoration."

"This one is like your wand," I said.

"My wand doesn't work anymore."

"It does," I said. "I promise."

"Keep moving for godsake," Earnest called down to us.

"Listen," I said to Anya. "Move up the road toward your dad. Tell him I'm gonna rally the last cow. The one that peeled off. Tell him I'm making a game-time decision, and tell him I'll bring her up to the pasture and then I'll find my way back to Lyle's. And tell him not to wait."

"That's far," she said. I considered the distance back to Lyle's and I knew she was right—it was far. But I kept that to myself. I thought then about Lyle's steady belief in me, the way he trusted me with his animals and farm when no one else in the world believed in me.

"It won't be too far if I cut across the fields," I said. "I kind of feel like running through pastures anyway." The moon cast a metallic glow. Anya looked up at me and then brought the buckeye close to her eyes. My legs and arms grew antsy, but I tried to keep it together. I plucked a long piece of grass and stuck it in my mouth.

"We could've been happy here," she said. Her knees moved back and forth. She kicked at the gravel. "That's what my dad used to say to my mom. But not anymore." She rubbed the buckeye and put it in her pocket. "Thank you," she said. She turned and started up the gravel, with her big jacket and skinny legs, her wand waving in the air.

●   ●   ●

I wasn't too worried about the cow. One seemed manageable. But I was worried about other things. My hands shook, and I felt that dull pain in my neck. I reached for the Mini-Maglite and tried it again. I shoved it back in my vest pocket. I bent down to re-lace my boots, and when Anya had gotten far enough away, I turned and ran into the rolling pastures, under the bright moon, keeping an eye out for that one cow.

When I was a ways out, running over uneven pasture, I decided to double back. I ran up along the fence line near the road. I got close to where Earnest had parked. I squatted behind a tree. Anya stood by the car, still waving her wand.

I could hear Earnest, somewhere in the dark, securing the pasture gate—the clanking chain latched onto the metal bars. And then he came back into focus, walking around the Olds to the passenger door. I steadied my breath, inhaling through my nose. My hands relaxed.

Earnest opened the door and the interior light came on. Anya was looking up at the moon, waving the wand above her head. "Go on now," he said to his daughter. Anya started toward the door, and as she walked closer to her dad he rested his hand on her shoulder and patted her back a couple of times and then pulled her close. "Happy birthday, darling," he said.

"Thanks, Daddy," she said. She crawled in and reached for the seatbelt. Earnest waited until she was secure, and then he closed the door gently and walked around the front of the car, his boots scuffing the gravel. I stayed hidden behind the tree, crouched low, and watched the red taillights light up the road and then disappear around the bluff.

And there I was, squatting in the dark with a cow to chase, and thoughts that would chase me for days. Who was I to think? How could I ever do this on my own?

ACKNOWLEDGEMENTS

Thank you a million times to the wonderful folks at *Midwestern Gothic*, especially Jeff Pfaller, Robert James Russell, and Michelle Webster-Hein. Thank you.

Thank you to my first writing teachers and earliest encouragers: Andrew Porter and Mary Kay Shanley at the Iowa Summer Writing Festival, and David Faldet and Amy Weldon at Luther College.

For their keen eye and rigorous support, I'd like to thank my dear friends and readers who have made these stories stronger versions of themselves: Bibi Deitz, John Domini, Libby Flores, Jay Hodges, Linda Michel-Cassidy, Ruth Mukwana, Joanne Proulx, Cassie Pruyn, Walter Robinson, Cathy Salibian, Corina Zappia, and especially Denton Loving.

A heartfelt thank you to the Bennington Writing Seminars, my second home, where I had the good fortune to work with Wesley Brown, David Gates, Amy Hempel, and Bret Anthony Johnston. Supreme teachers and mentors, all.

Thank you to the kind and generous editors at the following journals and magazines for their smart suggestions and editorial instincts: Nate Brown at *American Short Fiction*, A.J. Stoughton at *Columbia Review*, Renee LeClaire, Kristen Daily, and Debra Marquart at *Flyway*, Mark Drew at the *Gettysburg Review*, Jason Allen at *Harpur Palate*, Alison Penning and Jocelyn Sears at *Meridian*, Matt Socia at *Redivider*, Jen Porter and Alison Turner at *The Tishman Review*, and Celia Johnson, Maria Gagliano, and Beth Blachman at *Slice Magazine*.

Thank you to Ryan Collins and Sal Marici at the Midwest Writing Center. My week of solitude and writing in Rock Island allowed for the finishing touches.

Thank you to my friends at home, in Decorah, Iowa, who have supported me with laughter, beer, and literary conversation: Nancy Barry, David Grouws, Charlie Langton, Dirk Marple, June Melby, Cerrisa Snethen, Brett Steelman, and Amy Weldon. Also, a huge thank you to Kate Rattenborg and Kate Scott at Dragonfly Books, and everyone affiliated with the Arthaus. Finally, a hearty cheers to the midnight lane-walkers, Old Style drinkers, and best-Thanksgiving-dinner-ever friends of Book Group. Exemplary literary citizens, all.

Note: The title "Between the Fireflies" is taken from a song titled "Darkness Between the Fireflies" by Mason Jennings. Also, in that story, I use some of his song lyrics, though they have been rewritten slightly to suit the needs of the story. Thank you Mason Jennings for the conversation after the concert.

I cannot express enough the gratitude I have for my parents, David and Juliet, whose impact here is more than I'll ever be able to articulate. And thank you to my siblings for their confidence and belief.

Finally, thank you to Molly, Celia, Franklin, and Nora. For your support. For being there. For everything. This book is for you.

Keith Lesmeister was born in North Carolina, raised in Iowa, and received his M.F.A. from the Bennington Writing Seminars. His fiction has appeared in *American Short Fiction, Slice, Meridian, Redivider, Gettysburg Review*, and many other print and online publications. His nonfiction has appeared in *Tin House Open Bar, River Teeth, The Good Men Project*, and elsewhere. He currently lives in northeast Iowa where he teaches at Northeast Iowa Community College. *We Could've Been Happy Here* is his first book.